Horses of the Sun

The Outback Riders - 1

LEANNE OWENS

DEDICATION

For Chris – we were the Outback Riders of our day.
For our three children, Robert, Kate, and Michael.
For Miss Margaret Biviano, who taught me to love words.
For all those who have dreams – reach for them.

CONTENTS

CHAPTER ONE
I Hate Horses

'I say we put a snake in her bed – a king brown,' Matthew nodded meaningfully at his older brother and sister, his eyes serious as they discussed ways to upset the mysterious cousin who was about to visit and disrupt their lives.

Dane grinned at his brother. At fourteen, he was four years older than Matthew and one year older than their sister Lani, but sometimes he felt like an adult when they were carried away with crazy ideas, and it was left to him to be the voice of reason. They were sitting on his bed talking about the cousin they'd never met. She was coming from the city to live with them on their outback cattle station for a year while her parents worked overseas.

'We can't do something that will kill her, Matt,' he pointed out sensibly. 'She is family, after all. Think of something we can do that is funny but won't end in death, insanity, or loss of a leg.'

'Well, that makes it harder,' Matthew thought for a

moment. 'A dead snake in her bed?' He didn't mind if it was alive or dead; he just thought any prank involving a snake was a good idea.

Lani giggled, 'A legless lizard that looks like a snake.'

'A rubber snake and a handful of cockroaches,' Matthew chortled.

Unable to help himself, Dane joined in, 'The fake vomit Uncle John gave us on her pillow.'

Matthew dropped off the chair and rolled on his back on the floor, laughing uncontrollably, forcing words out between his howls, 'Stink beetles in her undies!'

'Itchy grubs in her jeans,' added Lani, 'and a bucket of frogs let loose in her room at night.'

'Spiders!' spurted Matthew. 'A bucket full of giant hairy spiders.'

'Good luck keeping the spiders in your bucket,' their mother interrupted dryly from the door, looking in to see her three children in an uproar about tricks to play on her only sister's only child. She smiled at them and thought, not for the first time, that she was lucky to have three children who knew how to laugh together. They were all lean and fit from their life outdoors. They had brown hair like hers, and the boys had their father's brown eyes while Lani had her deep green eyes. Her sister had sent her recent photos of her niece, and she shared a remarkable resemblance with Lani; they could easily pass as twins. 'And you will simply make her welcome – no spiders or dog poo or sheep let loose in her room.'

'Sheep in her room,' Matthew slapped the floor as he laughed, 'Good one, Mum. A couple of big old, smelly rams sitting there ready to butt her.'

'And you, Matthew,' she smiled sweetly at him, 'will have the job of cleaning up the results of any tricks played, as well as cleaning up the dishes for the next month if you play those tricks.'

That stopped his laughter. 'Aw, Mum, unfair.'

'No - fair. Your cousin Amy is going to have enough to cope with leaving her home and school friends behind, as well as her whole city lifestyle, and coming out here, without you making her feel unwanted and out of place.'

'She will be out of place,' Lani grumbled. 'Last time we had city kids stay, all they did was complain about everything and say how backward we are compared to the city.'

'I'm sure Amy will be different,' said her mother without much confidence. 'And, even if she's not, you will be nice to her because it can't be easy to be left with a family you don't even know while your parents go away for a year. Dad will have her here before long, so get your welcoming smiles ready – and glue them to your faces.' She finished with a narrow-eyed warning.

'Well, as long as she likes horses,' muttered Lani. 'If she doesn't like horses, she may as well curl up and die.'

'All girls like horses,' said Dane. 'She'll drive us nuts wanting to ride our horses.'

'She's not riding my horse,' declared Matthew, and then smirked as he looked around his family of riders who spent most of their spare time with horses. 'But I don't know what she'll do with herself around here if she doesn't like horses.'

An hour later, their cousin stood in their kitchen, looked around at her newly discovered family, and announced in a superior voice, 'I hate horses.'

The three Winter children stared at her. Amy was everything they had feared. She was dressed in expensive designer clothes with ridiculous shoes that may have cost a fortune but were useless on a cattle station, more make-up than a model, and her hair arranged like she was off to the races. She was thirteen, the same age as Lani, but she looked around at them as though she was grown up and they were annoying little children. They had barely finished their introductions before Matthew asked her about horses, resulting in that stunning announcement.

'All horses?' asked Matthew.

Amy moved her head slowly until she looked at Matthew; she narrowed her eyes and looked down her nose at him, 'I just told you I hate horses, didn't I? Unless you can show me a horse that isn't a horse, then I'm going to hate it because I hate horses. They smell bad, and they make stupid noises.'

'You don't have to like horses, Amy,' said her aunt kindly, trying to intervene before her three children started a fight with their cousin over the smells and noises of horses. 'Dane, Lani, and Matthew spend a lot of their time with them, but there are many things to do here that don't involve horses. What sort of things do you like doing?'

Amy looked out the window at the vast expanse of open plains country that stretched away endlessly from the homestead. It had taken over two hours of driving from the nearest town to reach Sunhaven Downs. Two hours of dusty, bumpy dirt roads with kangaroos, cattle, and sheep scattered around on the brown, unfenced grass. If ever there was a 'middle of nowhere,' she decided, this was it.

'I like to shop.'

The three Winter children snorted at her response. Their mother silenced them with a harsh glance.

'It's a long way to the shops from here, Amy,' Mrs. Winter smiled at her, 'but you can shop online if you like. We order a lot of our things over the internet, so you can still buy anything you want, just without the walking-into-the-shops part. Perhaps you'll learn to like horses while you're here. We have some lovely quiet ponies that you could learn on.'

'I told you, I don't like horses,' Amy replied fiercely, looking at her aunt with such rudeness that her cousins wanted to slap her. 'I didn't want to come here in the first place, and I don't want anything to do with your stupid horses. '

Eleanor Winter breathed deeply before replying, reminding herself that her niece didn't know them. It would be traumatic for her to stay with a family she'd never met so that her mother and step-father could go overseas without her. Two days ago, this girl had been in her city home in Melbourne, surrounded by everything familiar, and now she was with strangers after traveling thousands of kilometers north.

Perhaps, Eleanor hoped, she was so exhausted and worn out that she was simply cranky with tiredness, and some rest time might reveal a well-mannered, likable girl. At least, Eleanor told herself, that was what she hoped. If not, it was going to be a long three weeks of September school holidays before Dane and Lani went back to boarding school, taking Amy with them for her first taste of being a boarder. Matthew stayed home as he still learned with Distance Education, the home-schooling system commonly used in the outback

'Do you play any sports?' Her aunt smiled at her. 'You look athletic – tennis or basketball, perhaps?'

'I used to do gymnastics,' she replied in a stiff voice.

'Gymnasts should make good riders,' suggested Lani cheerfully.

'Yes, I can see the similarity,' Amy said, sarcasm

dripping from her words. 'Cartwheels and somersaults across the floor look exactly like trying to sit in a saddle.'

'Why don't I show you to your room, Amy,' Mrs. Winter quickly intervened before Lani had a chance to reply. 'We can settle you in before we have dinner. Perhaps you'd like a shower.'

'I prefer baths,' stated Amy with what sounded like a sniff of disgust at the thought of a shower.

'It's a drought,' snapped Lani, 'and we only have short showers to save water – none of your fifteen-minute city showers.'

Amy gave Lani a withering look, 'I guess I should be thankful you don't have dust baths.'

Before Lani could snap back or move in to hit her cousin, Mrs. Winter took Amy's shoulder and ushered her out of the kitchen, 'Your room is this way, Amy. I hope you'll like it.'

'Better take all the horse stuff out of there, Mum or Amy might faint at the sight of it,' called Lani as a parting shot. She was usually a friendly girl who welcomed strangers to their outback home, but looking at her cousin was like looking in a weird mirror where the reflection was a pretentious, town version of herself. She disliked both the similarities and the differences.

'There are quite a few posters of horses as well as books and horse trophies and sashes in your room,' apologized Mrs. Winter to her niece. 'Why don't you pack away anything you don't want and make your room the way you like.'

'It won't worry me, Aunt Eleanor,' Amy shrugged. 'It's not like it's my room. The horse stuff can stay.'

'It is your room, and you can rearrange it any way you like. Have a look around the house when you feel ready. It was built over a hundred years ago, and all the bedrooms and bathrooms are along this side. The dining room, lounge, office, games room, kitchen, and everything else along that side, with this big corridor in between, so it's easy to find your way around. The veranda runs around the whole lot, and in summer, we often move beds out there, but everything is air-conditioned if you want to stay cool in your room.'

Amy didn't say anything; she just stood looking bored, leaving her aunt wishing that she and Kristy, Amy's mother, hadn't grown so distant. She knew nothing of her niece. Kristy had dropped her into their lives for a year without explaining anything about her apart from the fact that she thought they'd all get on well. She'd added that her new husband, Nikos, believed it was important for Amy to know her family. Amy wanted to stay with friends while her parents were away, but Nikos refused to leave his stepdaughter behind with friends when she had a family.

'I know it might be a bit difficult getting used to a horsey family when you don't like them yourself, but I'm sure we'll cope. I'm afraid your mother and I were never very close, and when she became an archaeologist and I went nursing, we just drifted further apart. We became so busy with our own lives that we didn't take enough interest in each other's lives. I should have made an effort to visit and get to know you before you were thirteen. Will you forgive me and give me a chance to get to know you now?'

Amy paused outside the open door of her new bedroom and looked at her aunt without any expression in her eyes, 'I don't know why you'd want to. I'm only here for a few weeks, and then I'm off to boarding school.'

Mrs. Winter wrapped her arms around Amy. 'You're my niece, my sister's child,' she whispered as the girl stood stiff and unresponsive in her arms. 'Of course, I want to get to know you. Everyone out here goes to boarding school at your age. It's not a punishment. It's just what we do out here. I'm sure you'll learn to like it.'

Amy pulled away from her aunt and asked coolly, 'What time is dinner? I might have a rest and change out of these clothes before then.'

'Six o'clock,' Mrs. Winter looked sadly at her niece. She was such an unemotional child who seemed empty of all joy. 'I'll come and remind you ten minutes before then in case you've fallen asleep. You have your own bathroom, so you won't have to share, and if you want to go outside for a look around, the door on the other side of your bedroom opens onto the veranda and the gardens.'

'Thank you,' Amy said, turning away from her aunt and entering the large bedroom where Uncle Geoff had placed her suitcases. She shut the door firmly behind her, cutting her aunt off before she could say anything else.

Eleanor stared at the closed door, wondering how she would manage to reach this hard-edged urban girl who looked so out of place in the outback.

'She's just tired and worn out,' Mrs. Winter held her hand up at her children when she returned to the kitchen. 'Don't make any judgments yet, and don't whine to me about her.'

'But, Mum,' began Matthew.

'Don't *but Mum* me, Matthew,' she looked at him severely. 'Amy has traveled to what must seem like another world – give her a chance. And don't annoy her about horses.'

The three Winter children pulled faces at each other and headed out into the garden so that they could talk about their cousin.

8

In her bedroom, Amy stood for a long moment staring at the horse posters and trophies and sashes that lined the walls. Champion Stock Horse. Supreme Thoroughbred Exhibit. Champion Girl Rider. Supreme Exhibit of the Show. Western Polocrosse Championships – A Grade Winners. There were hundreds of sashes and trophies; all won at horse events. Photos of the family with their horses and wins proved that all the Winters competed and won. Horses, horses, everywhere. 'Horses of the Sun' was written on many of the photos, as that seemed to be the name given to the Sunhaven horses.

Amy sat on the bed and buried her face in her hands, and began to cry. She curled up on the bed and pushed her face into the pillow to smother the sound of her sobs because she was determined to keep her secrets hidden from the Winters. She was still in shock about the sudden change in her life. Two weeks ago, she had so much to look forward to, she had her sights set on the Olympics in six years, and she was prepared to work her heart out to get there, and she knew she would make it.

Her step-father announced that he and her mother were going to Turkey to work for a year, and she would live with a family she knew nothing about. Her mother never spoke of them – if something was outside her archaeology work, it may as well not have existed. There were no Christmas cards, or phone calls, no photos. Amy didn't even know she had three cousins who rode horses until two weeks ago.

She had begged, raged, and cried, but her parents ripped her away from everything she loved. There was nothing she could do about it except watch her dreams disappear. Her heart was breaking, but she wasn't going to let any of these horse people know anything about it. Her shattered dreams remained her secrets – she would not share them with a family of outback horse riders.

CHAPTER TWO
I Hate Her

Dinner was a strained affair. Mr. and Mrs. Winter asked Amy about her family and interests, and she answered in as few words as possible. Lani tried to make conversation by asking about what music and movies she liked, something she thought all city kids would be interested in, but only received a shrug as a reply. Dane asked about what sort of computer games she liked and received a cool look and a statement that she didn't waste her time on computers. Matthew didn't even bother to attempt conversation after seeing his brother and sister shut down by this uppity city girl.

After dinner, they went for a walk around the garden. Hundreds of solar-powered lights along paths, amongst the flowers and shrubs, and in the trees lit up the gardens so that they looked magical. The lawn wound between flowers and flowering shrubs, and a scattering of tall trees provided various outlines against the starry sky. The small lights throughout the garden and plants made it look like

11

the Milky Way had come to rest there. Amy appeared unmoved by the beauty of it.

'Isn't this the best garden you've ever seen at night?' asked Lani as she gazed around at the garden.

'Not bad. I've seen better.' Amy replied calmly.

'Well, I think it's the best even if it's not up to *your* standards,' Lani snipped, offended that their cousin dismissed the enchantment of the Sunhaven gardens so quickly.

'Why don't the three of you show Amy the games room,' suggested their father, catching the tense situation between the children and trying to suggest something that they could enjoy together without arguing. 'You can play the computer or X-box or whatever else is there, Amy, and I'm telling you,' he grinned, 'I think the kids have everything. Or you can play snooker or darts or put some music on and dance.'

'Dad,' Lani looked mortified at his suggestions, 'we don't dance in the games room.'

'I'd rather go to bed early,' sniffed Amy, looking at each of her cousins in such a way as to imply she would prefer to do nothing by herself than anything with them. 'What time should I get up in the morning.'

'We get up at first light,' Mr. Winter told her, 'but you're welcome to sleep-in. I don't imagine you're used to getting up very early in the city.'

Amy's lips narrowed at her uncle's words thinking he may have been insulting her city upbringing, but he wasn't, so she shrugged, one of her most common responses to any comments directed at her urban life.

'Goodnight, dear,' Mrs. Winter once more tried to hug her niece, only to be met with coolness. 'Give us a call if you want anything. Help yourself to any food or drink in

HORSES OF THE SUN

the kitchen if you get hungry during the night.'

'I hate her,' growled Lani once her cousin was out of earshot. 'She's a stuck-up cow who thinks she's so much better than us, and she's rude.'

'Settle, petal,' their father scruffed Lani's hair. 'Give her a chance. I'm sure you'll all get along fine.'

'Put up with this settling in period,' Mrs. Winter assured the children without feeling very confident about the truth of her words, 'and once she feels more at home here and finds her own space, everything will be different. Alright? Just be nice until then.'

The children agreed half-heartedly and remained on the lawn as their parents went inside. As soon as they saw their parents climb the steps onto the house, Dane motioned with his head to follow him. The three of them headed to their Meeting Room in the back corner of the garden, a small wooden shed hidden in their parent's Rainforest Grove. They pushed past palm fronds and tropical plants, which their mother had struggled to keep alive during the drought, and entered the shed, switching on the battery-powered lantern and seating themselves on the three chairs around the old wooden table. It used to be their cubby house, but they felt they'd outgrown that name, so now called it their Meeting Room.

'I knew I should have put a snake in her bed,' said Matthew. 'And it should have been a king brown, and he should have been very alive and angry.'

'She'd have bitten it and killed it,' grumbled Lani. 'Poor snake.'

'She does seem venomous,' agreed Dane.

Lani shook her head, 'I can't see why her parents would send her here – she hates horses, she likes shopping, and she looks like she's allergic to the outdoors. It must be her worst nightmare. Did they hate her?'

'I overheard Mum and Dad talking about that,' Dane spoke softly so that his voice didn't carry across the garden. 'Her mum – the aunt we've never met – and her step-father have gone to Turkey for a dig.' Seeing the question in Matthews's eyes, he explained, 'It's what archaeologists call the place where they're digging up the past. Anyway, her Dad died about five years ago, and it seems we're her only family. It's supposed to be dangerous in Turkey, and Aunt Kristy wanted to make sure Amy was with family in case they never came back.'

Matthew looked horrified at the thought of something happening to Amy's mother, 'You mean, we could be stuck with her forever?'

'Better pray for safe conditions in Turkey, eh, Matty?' grinned Dane.

'I'll do more than pray,' he declared, thumping the table with a fist. 'I'm telling you - I'm emailing their leader tonight to beg him to keep Aunt Kristy safe so she can come back and rescue us from her daughter. Her funeral would be our funeral.'

'She'll come back.' Dane told him. 'We only have to put up with her for a year, and most of that is at boarding school,' he gave Lani a wicked glance and chuckled. 'Lani will have her all year, but you and me, bro, it's school holidays only.'

Matthew laughed and pointed at his sister, 'You're going to have to show her around school and be all nice to her there for the rest of the year. Suffer!'

Screwing up her nose at him, she shrugged, 'Whatever. Let's worry about tomorrow first. Want to draw straws to see who has to show her around the place?' Lani held up two long straws and a short straw.

'Nah, I'll do it,' Dane sacrificed himself. 'I'm the oldest, so it's my job to try and protect you from the dragon. You two work the horses, and I'll be the good cousin who shows her where everything is.'

They continued talking, unaware of Amy quietly returning to the house from outside the Meeting Room. She hadn't meant to eavesdrop, but she'd seen her cousins heading into the corner of the garden as she watched from her bedroom window and decided to follow to see what they were doing. Over-hearing them discuss the possibility of her mother dying overseas and never returning sent chills through her. She'd tried not to think of it, but she knew it could happen. The last place she wanted to grow up was here, in the wilds of the outback, with three horse-mad cousins who called her a dragon.

She smiled to herself, the first smile she'd had in days, as she thought of just how much of a dragon she could become. Winter children, she thought as she began planning ways to make their lives hell, your nightmare is about to begin.

What Amy didn't realize was that a person could not change their nature as easily as that, and she was not by nature a nasty person. Her true character would shine when faced with three of the Winters dying before the week was out, and the events would change them all, forever.

CHAPTER THREE
I Won't Ride a Horse

Everyone had finished breakfast and started their chores when Amy wandered into the kitchen on her first morning at Sunhaven. She sat down alone at the large table in the middle of the enormous room, and as Lani walked past with the vegetable scraps to feed the chooks, she demanded breakfast.

'I like an omelet for breakfast, thank you, with warm – not hot - chocolate milk.'

Lani stopped to stare at her cousin, dressed in a flowing buttercup yellow skirt, white silk shirt, and pretty sandals, with her hair carefully arranged and make-up applied. Sunhaven was a place for sensible work clothes, like her shorts, t-shirt, boots, and socks, with an Akubra on her head for sun protection, not race-day clothes.

'Ah, good morning, and get it yourself,' Lani said with a pointed look. 'You'll find everything you need in the fridge and cupboards. I had breakfast an hour ago with everyone else, and now I have chores to finish so I can go and work my horse.'

'Where's my aunt and uncle? Why doesn't Aunt Eleanor get breakfast for me?' asked Amy in a petulant voice. 'I shouldn't have to feed myself – I'm your guest.'

'Guests feed themselves around here,' said Lani through clenched teeth, annoyed by this vision of loveliness expecting to be waited on as though she was at a resort. 'Mum is feeding the horses because they need help getting breakfast from the feed room; you don't. And Dad has taken Matthew to check the waters.'

'Check the waters?'

'Check the water supply,' explained Dane, who entered the kitchen at that point and received a grateful smile from his sister as she went on her way, leaving him with their cousin. 'They drive around to check the dams, bores, and troughs to make sure all the stock have a good water supply. We check the waters a couple of times a week.'

'When will they be back?'

'It takes a few hours to do the western run and another three hours for the eastern run. Driving to each watering-place in every paddock works out to be about two hundred kilometers with lots of gates to open.'

Amy looked surprised. She knew that Sunhaven was big, but to drive two hundred kilometers around it without leaving seemed incredible.

'Once you have breakfast, I can take you for a drive to see some of it, if you like,' he offered.

'You're only fourteen; you can't drive,' she gave him a withering look. 'It's against the law.'

'We all drive. Even Matthew's been driving for years. It's no big deal; every kid out here can. We don't drive on government roads, and we're not breaking any laws driving on our place. We can all drive cars, motorbikes, tractors, trucks, even the bulldozer and front-end loader.'

She looked doubtful as though she was unsure if he was joking with her or not, then asked where she could find something for breakfast. Dane showed her the large walk-in pantry that looked to have several years' food supply and opened the cupboards and drawers for the plates and cutlery.

'Help yourself,' he told her. 'When you're ready, I'll be outside in the shed where we keep the cars, and I'll show you a bit of Sunhaven.'

'I'd rather wait for Aunt Eleanor or Uncle Geoff. I don't think it's safe for fourteen-year-old boys to drive.'

He shrugged, 'Tough. Get used to it.'

'Or not,' she glared at him as she poured some milk from a jug over her cornflakes. Sniffing the milk, she wrinkled up her nose, 'This smells odd – and why does it have darker colored milk floating on top?'

'It's fresh milk, from a cow – that's cream on the top. We don't have a local supermarket - we milk our own cows.'

The jug thumped down on the bench, and Amy sat her bowl of cereal and milk on the sink with a look of disgust, 'Ugh, I could have been poisoned. I only drink milk that comes in containers from a shop.'

'It comes in containers,' grinned Dane, amused that his cousin hadn't seen fresh milk before. 'They're called udders – the mammary glands of cows. I milked that lot yesterday with my own hands,' he held up his hands, and his grin broadened as he saw the look of distaste spread over her face. 'Yep, pulled all that milk out of the teats with my own hot little hands. And when the milk cools and settles, the cream rises to the top. You have to stir it before using, or you'll get a bowl of cream.'

'How repulsive. Don't you have any milk in a bottle?'

'Only if you pour that milk into a bottle. Hey, it tastes good – you'll get used to it.'

'I'll get used to eating toast for breakfast,' Amy grumbled, putting the milk jug back in the fridge. 'I suppose you made bread with your own hands, too?'

'There are a few dozen loaves left in the freezer in the pantry,' he told her. 'We only go shopping every few weeks, or not for a month or more in the wet season, so we always have a heap of it in the freezer.'

'Good bread or just the cheap, white, unhealthy stuff?' she regarded him with aversion, clearly implying that she expected her outback family to have the cheap bread. 'I prefer wholemeal with wholegrain, of course.'

'Of course, you do,' Dane nodded at her as he leaned against the bench, amused by her attempts to insult his family over what bread they ate. He wanted to go outside as he intended, but it was fun sparring with her. She was the most annoying person he had ever met.

'And fresh. We get our bread fresh every morning from the local bakery. This bread is…' she glanced at the date tag on the pack of bread she just pulled from the freezer, 'four months old! Four months!' She shook the bag at him, 'What sort of people eat bread that is four months old?'

Dane scowled at her, a little irritated by that remark, 'It's been frozen all that time – it's not like it's covered in mold and maggots.'

Amy shot him a dirty look, 'I wouldn't be surprised what was on food around here if you only go shopping every few weeks. I used to go shopping every day when I could. We never ate old food in our house.'

'Get used to it,' shrugged Dane, setting the toaster on the bench for her to use. 'Instead of shopping every day, you'll just have to get used to what's outside this house – and it's not a city.'

'I can see that,' Amy sniffed, 'but I don't have to like it. Do you do anything for fun around here that doesn't involve horses?'

'We swim in the dam and the turkey's nest at the big bore,' he said. Seeing her raised brows at the unfamiliar terms and being helpful by nature, he explained, 'A turkey's nest is like a raised circle of dirt that holds water. Bores are places where we've drilled down to get underground water. Our main bore pumps into a turkey's nest that's about the size of a big pool, and it's great for swimming, even in winter, because the water's hot where the bore runs in.'

'I only swim at the beach or in pools that are chlorinated,' Amy announced stiffly as she spread butter and honey on her toast. 'I don't swim in dirty water.'

He ignored her and continued, 'We go fishing sometimes and catch crawchies.'

'Crawchies?'

'I think you call them yabbies in Victoria,' he waited to see that she understood that term for the small freshwater crayfish. 'We go pig shooting to get rid of some of the feral pigs. And we go to dances and shoots – clay target shooting days – and parties on weekends when we're not working or at some horse event. If you learn to ride a horse, you'll always have something to do.'

'I won't ride a horse,' she grimaced at the thought. 'So, I guess I'll be reading a lot of books and sitting around by myself as I'm not into hunting animals, shooting animals, catching animals on hooks, or getting on top of animals and riding them around.' She groaned and rolled her eyes, 'I can't believe that my mother thought I could spend the year here in the wilderness with this Wild West outfit rather than stay with friends in the city.'

'Yeah, does seem a bit strange,' drawled Dane, fighting his desire to walk away from his rude cousin. He tried to see things from her point of view, 'I don't think I'd like to spend a year in the city away from all this.'

'All this?' Amy raised her brows and looked out the window. 'It's just a great emptiness. There's no *all this* about flat, boring paddocks that go on forever.'

'You haven't seen the Sunhaven Hills, though – they're not flat or boring.' Dane was growing tired of how she tried to insult everything about his home, land, and lifestyle, and it was becoming harder to remain pleasant to her.

'You're kidding,' Amy shook her head. 'You think a couple of hills are going to excite me?'

'Finish your breakfast, and I'll take you for a look. It's ten minutes in the car, and then you can climb up and see the view. You can see the curve of the earth from the top.'

'You know you can't see the curve of the earth from any point on the ground.'

'It seems that way when you're on the top of the hills.'

'Well, you can't, and I don't want to climb to the top of your hills,' Amy ungraciously declined his offer. 'I think I'll have a look around the garden after breakfast. Maybe get on the computer and catch up with my friends… if they're not out having a good time shopping.'

Dane shrugged, 'Just trying to make you feel welcome here, but, hey, if you are dead set on hating it, I can't help with that. Use the computer in the games room, if you like.' He turned and left the house.

'Yeah, well, better luck next time with sacrificing yourself to the dragon,' Amy muttered as he left, too softly for him to hear as she didn't want him to know she had been listening outside their cubby house the night before.

22

'I hope I make your lives as miserable as mine because you have no idea what I've lost by coming here.'

Tears pricked her eyes when she allowed herself to think of everything she'd been forced to leave behind by being sent to this place and all the dreams that had shattered when her mother coldly swept them aside and told her she had no choice in the matter. She quickly wiped her eyes and focussed on ways to annoy her cousins. She smiled. Irritating them would make her feel better.

CHAPTER FOUR
The First Four Days

Dane went outside, relieved to escape the harping negativity of his cousin. Knowing that Lani would have finished her chores by now and be with the horses, he headed to the stables. The buildings of Sunhaven were set in a square arrangement, with the homestead and gardens on one side, the main machinery shed along the next side, the stable block and horse yards on the side opposite the home, and a couple of cottages and jackaroo quarters for the workers on the fourth side. The couple who worked on Sunhaven and the two station-hands were on holiday, so the cottages were empty.

At the stables, Dane found his sister grooming her grey polocrosse horse, Fleet, and she had his bay mare, Misty, tied outside her stable, waiting to be brushed. He looked beyond the stables to see his mother on Captain with a polocrosse ball and racquet, which was a bit like a net on the end of a stick, practicing some moves on the large riding arena. As Captain spun and slid, small clouds of dust rose around his hooves, reminding him of how dry it was for the ninth year in a row.

'How'd it go with city-kid?' Lani asked as she finished with the brush and tossed it to Dane.

'Unbelievable,' he laughed and shook his head. 'I mean, un-blinking-believe-able. She is about as friendly as that snake Matthew wanted to put in her bed and doesn't miss a chance to run us all down.'

'So, not taking her for a drive this morning, then?' she grinned at him and began saddling Fleet.

'Nah, we skipped on that – she's going to get on the computer and complain to her friends about us. No matter, I'll do some practice with you and Mum, then you can try and entertain her 'cause I'm done trying to make her feel welcome, for today, anyway.'

'Yeah, looking forward to that – not.' Lani pulled a face. 'Maybe she'd like to bake a cake or go for a walk.'

They continued to chat as they put the stock saddles on their horses, bandaged their legs for protection, and put the snaffle bridles on before clipping on their helmets and leading the horses into the sunshine to mount them. After five minutes of walking and trotting to warm them up, Dane cantered back to the stables to pick up their two racquets leaning against the wall. He tossed one to Lani, who caught it deftly and started swinging it around, testing the weight.

'Catch!' Mrs. Winter called to Lani as she cantered past on her big black horse, Captain.

She flicked the soft polocrosse ball out of her racquet. Lani spun Fleet around to be in the correct position to snap her racquet through the air and catch the ball with a satisfying *thwuck* as it landed in the net. Touching Fleet's sides lightly, Lani set him in a canter alongside Captain, and they tossed the ball back and forth until Dane called for it. Lani turned around to see Misty coming up the arena at a hand gallop.

'Keep coming fast!' she told him, throwing the ball to a spot well ahead of her brother. At the speed he was traveling, he intercepted the ball perfectly, swung it around in his racquet, and flicked it out through the goalposts.

'Another goal for world champions, Dane and Misty!' he whooped as he cantered a circle around his sister.

'Just luck,' she grinned at him.

'Then I'll score another ten lucky goals before you have one,' he laughed.

Mrs. Winter cantered over to the ball which had rolled far beyond the goalposts and leaned down to scoop it up in her racquet without slowing. She headed back to the center of the field with Lani alongside her, hitting her racquet to dislodge the ball, but skillful cradling kept it in the net.

From the corner of the veranda where Amy stood, she could see her cousins and aunt practicing. She watched for several minutes, fascinated despite her declared hatred of horses. Even someone who knew nothing about horses could see how well they could all ride. They were at home in the saddle, riding as one with their horses. At one point, Dane's horse lowered his head and threw in some high-spirited bucks, but her cousin just laughed and gave the horse a gentle slap on the neck and kept playing. She almost regretted her *I hate horses* stance but turned away before she could think any more along those lines.

The games room occupied one corner of the house. She went in and turned on a computer on one of the tables. As it warmed up, she looked around at the walls, covered in sashes, trophies, and photos of the Winter family wins at horse events. One picture caught her eye – her Uncle Geoff sitting on a big chestnut horse with the name 'Lord Sunhaven' written underneath. He looked like a horse that could win the Melbourne Cup, and she wondered if he was a racehorse.

The computer chirped that it was ready, and she sat down, opened Facebook, and logged in as Amity Fielding-King rather than Amy King, the name by which her cousins knew her. Her friends and family called her Amy, and though she usually shortened her name to King, she used her father's hyphenated name when she competed. That way, she wasn't one of any number of people with the last name of King in the results - she was the only Fielding-King.

'In outback Queensland,' she wrote. 'I saw a million kangaroos and two million sheep and cattle. It's a wide brown land, but it's not for me. Wishing I was home. I'm working on a way to get there.'

Within a few minutes of posting, there were a dozen *likes*, and friends began replying and asking about Sunhaven Downs. For the first time in days, she felt at ease as she chatted to friends about the trip to the outback and her first day there, keeping the public information quite neutral while revealing her true state of mind to a few close friends in private messages. She wished her mum would use her phone to send her a message, but she had said she would be out of contact for at least a week as they trekked to the remote area of the dig, so there was no way to communicate with her.

She was still typing to friends over an hour later when Dane and Lani found her. As soon as she heard them behind her, she logged off and shut the window. She didn't want them to see her friends' names because she didn't

28

want the questions that would follow. Some of her friends were well known, and she didn't want to explain to her cousins why a girl who hated horses was friends with some of the top athletes in the country, including riders.

'We're having smoko in the garden,' Lani informed her. 'Come and have something to eat and drink.'

The three of them walked in silence to where Mrs. Winter had set up morning tea on a table in the shade of a tree. There was orange juice, water, and a pot of tea, as well as a plate of cakes. Amy had to admit it did look inviting.

'No rain today,' Mrs. Winter made small talk as they took their seats and accepted drinks and cakes. 'There are supposed to be storms coming later in the week, so hopefully, we'll have some green grass to show Amy before the school holidays are over.'

Amy couldn't imagine the scorched brown land taking on green colors. It looked like it was on its way to becoming a desert.

'At least this heat makes for good swimming weather,' Mrs. Winter continued. 'Lani might take you down to the creek for a swim later, if you like, Amy.'

With a cool glance at her cousin, Amy replied, 'I don't think so.'

Behind her mother's back, Lani pulled a face at Amy, who merely stared at her as though regarding something unpleasant on the bottom of her shoe.

'Did you do much swimming at home in Victoria?' Aunt Eleanor asked her, trying to find a topic that would allow Amy to talk despite her apparent aversion to conversation.

Amy tried to keep her answers to any questions as brief as possible, but she soon found herself beginning to thaw as the warmth of her aunt shone on her. Her mother had always been quite cool and distant, providing everything Amy needed to be successful in life and proud of her achievements, but she was always too busy with her own life and career to sit and spend time with her. She was too obsessed with work to show the unconditional love that Aunt Eleanor seemed to lavish on all those around her. Even a cranky, unpleasant niece dropped on them without warning was treated with such pleasantness that Amy could almost tell her aunt the truth. Almost.

'I know you didn't want to go out with Dane this morning, Amy, but I want Lani to go down to the cattle yards to check on the weaners we have there at the moment, and I'd like you to go with her. We usually have other people here to do some of these jobs, but during the school holidays, they often go home, and we all have to work to get the jobs done.'

It was difficult to deny her aunt's request after she had been so caring towards her. After they tidied up the dishes, she joined Lani at the front of the house.

Lani looked at Amy's pretty skirt, blouse, and sandals, more suited to a day out shopping than walking down a dusty road to check some cattle, and shook her head. 'Those clothes are too good,' she told her bluntly. 'Put them away for a day when we go to town, and go put some work clothes on.'

Amy gave a delicate shudder at the words and repeated, 'Work clothes?' as though Lani had asked her to lie down and roll in horse manure.

'If you don't have any with you, you can wear some of my things,' Lani offered without much enthusiasm. 'We look to be the same size, and I have lots of shorts and spare shoes.'

'Why can't I wear these?' asked Amy, twirling around,

so her skirt spun out into a beautiful wave of yellow around her. 'It's so pretty, don't you think?'

'Yeah, well, whatever,' Lani shrugged. 'The cows aren't going to appreciate it, but the burrs will. You'll get lots of burrs stuck to it. I just thought you'd rather not have it ruined. And you need shoes. There are burrs, prickles, centipedes, spiders, and snakes, and your sandals aren't going to protect you from any of them.'

Amy sighed dramatically, 'So, I should ditch my good fashion sense - which is very good, not that you'd know hidden away out here in the wilds.' She smiled inwardly at the storm brewing on Lani's face. 'Instead, I should favor practical, safe, and boring fashion. It will hurt to do this, but I'll go and change into *work clothes*, as you call them.'

Within minutes she returned in denim shorts, sneakers, and a resigned expression, and they set off on foot for the cattle yards, a few hundred meters from the homestead. As they walked along the dusty track, Lani attempted to talk about life on Sunhaven, but Amy was as disagreeable as possible. They ended up walking in silence, with Lani wishing her cousin wasn't such a pain, and Amy pleased that she'd annoyed Lani into silence.

When they reached the yards, a maze of high railed fences with shade trees in the corners, Amy was shocked by the amount of dust rising from the hooves of almost two hundred young cattle that were being weaned from their mothers. She covered her mouth and coughed as Lani skipped off to check the water troughs. As Lani topped up the hay feeders, she explained a few things as simply as possible in case her cousin had any interest at all in the running of the station. Amy didn't seem to want to learn anything about life on Sunhaven.

The walk back was silent after Amy grumbled a few

times about the dust on her clothes and in her hair. Lani finally told her to stop whinging and start finding things to enjoy rather than complaining about everything.

Amy had no intention of enjoying her outback experience, and spent the next few days avoiding doing anything with her cousins. They went about their holidays as though Amy wasn't there, working their horses, driving out to check on stock and fences, swimming in the dam, and handling the foals which had been born after foaling season began on the first of August. Anything that involved horses was guaranteed to keep Amy as far away as possible, so Dane, Lani, and Matthew enjoyed as much time as they could with their horses. It meant they didn't have to worry about their city cousin complaining about everything around her and telling them how much better life was in Melbourne.

The three Winters met once a day in the Meeting Room to grumble about how their spoiled and annoying cousin was ruining their holidays. They tried to be pleasant at mealtimes when they were in the same room as her because their parents watched over them like hawks. In their Meeting Room, they were free to say anything they wanted about the sullen and disagreeable Amy.

For her part, Amy tried to be as offensive as possible, though she found it hard to be rude to her aunt and uncle because they remained tolerant of her bad attitude and were always pleasant and understanding. She knew she was driving her cousins crazy and enjoyed the game of irritating them whenever she could. Each morning, she managed to hide the evidence of her nightly tears and put her sadness aside as she started the day with the aim of making life unpleasant for her cousins. She hoped that after a few weeks of this, the family might be open to her idea of returning to live with friends in Victoria and going back to her old school.

On the fifth day of Amy's visit, Mrs. Winter decided to force the issue of horses with her niece. If Amy could learn to ride a horse, it would make outback life so much more enjoyable for everyone. It wasn't as if Amy was physically allergic to horses; she just disliked them. Mrs. Winter felt sure that she could overcome that if she had the opportunity to discover how much fun it could be to explore Sunhaven on horseback. She had no inkling that Amy's ability to ride a horse would save her life in just a few days.

CHAPTER FIVE
Amy's First Ride

After breakfast on Amy's fifth day on Sunhaven, Mrs. Winter called her niece outside to show her a plump brown mare called Melly saddled up and standing patiently. Amy's eyes narrowed when she saw the mare as she guessed what her aunt wanted.

'I don't want to ride,' she said firmly. 'if I were meant to ride a horse, I would have been born with my behind in the shape of a saddle.'

'Nonsense, Amy. You've had several days to settle in, and you're living like you're not even here. You need to learn how to ride a horse so you can take part in more things around Sunhaven. I promise you, Melly is the sweetest, kindest horse you could ever wish for, and once you learn how to handle her, you'll enjoy life here so much more. She's quiet for a beginner, but don't let that fool you - she was a very successful show jumper once. As you learn and improve, you'll find she will match your ability. She can be yours, and when you know how to ride, you can saddle her up yourself and go out riding whenever you want.'

'Which would be never,' said Amy dryly.

'I've asked Matthew to help you,' her aunt continued, ignoring her complaints and smiling at Matthew, who came approached on his horse, Shandy. 'He'll explain anything you need to know once you're out riding. I know he's only ten, but he's a natural-born teacher. Today, you are just going to walk down to the cattle yards and back on the horses. You'll work it out easily. Pull the left rein to go left, right rein to go right, and both reins to stop. Squeeze with your legs to make her go forward. It's that easy. If you make mistakes, Melly will probably stop as that is her favorite pace.'

'I don't want to get on a horse. I'll look stupid,' she pouted.

'We all do when we start riding, dear, and if we ever start thinking that we look pretty darned good on a horse, you can guarantee the horse will buck us off or do something to remind us not to be so cocky around them. That's the way of horses. Be humble with them, love them, and love spending time with them.'

'See, Aunt Eleanor, that gives me three strikes and out just there. I'm not humble with them, I don't love them, and I won't like spending time with them.'

'You'll learn,' Mrs. Winter smiled at her and began fastening a helmet on her head. 'Always wear one of these when you ride.'

Amy pushed her aunt's hands away and pulled the helmet off, 'I don't want to wear someone else's smelly helmet – it could have lice.' She glared at Matthew as she spoke, leaving him with no doubt she meant he could have lice. He grinned at her and slowly raised a hand to scratch his head.

'I promise you, you'll enjoy it,' said Mrs. Winter.

'You can't possibly know what I'd enjoy,' snapped Amy, determined to stay away from the horse.

'Stop being so rude to my mum,' declared Matthew, who rode Shandy forward and angrily stared down at his cousin. 'Stop behaving like a spoiled princess and just put the helmet on and get on the horse. You don't have to like it, Amy, just do it.'

'She's alright, Matthew,' said Mrs. Winter gently, trying to calm him.

'No, she's not, Mum,' Matthew replied. 'I don't care that she's rude to the three of us. It's obvious she doesn't like us and doesn't want to be here, but she should treat you better. Stop whinging, Amy, get on the horse, and don't be rude to my Mum again.'

Amy glared up at her cousin, 'I told you I don't want to get on the horse.' She had the grace to give her aunt an apologetic look and added, 'But I am sorry to sound rude to you, Aunt Eleanor. I really, really don't want to have anything to do with horses.'

'Horses are in your blood, Amy, if you'll just give them a chance,' Mrs. Winter told her soothingly. 'Your mother was the only one in the family who wasn't horse-mad, but your grandparents and great grandparents were all excellent horse people. Just give it a chance, and I think you'll find that you'll be a natural. I'll have Melly saddled up here every day until you agree to get on her and go for a ride.'

For a moment, Amy gritted her teeth and looked as though she would do as they asked. She looked Melly in the eyes and stretched her hand out so that the horse could touch it with her muzzle.

'Just stop being a chicken and get on her,' Matthew urged. 'She's dead quiet, and by the end of the holidays, you'll be riding like a champion.'

Melly exhaled warm breath over Amy's hand and, without warning, she turned on her heels and ran to her bedroom. She couldn't face getting on that horse. She couldn't let her cousin and aunt see the emotions she was working so hard to hide. Once in her bedroom, she threw herself on the bed and gave in to the tears.

After instructing Matthew to wait with the horses, Mrs. Winter went to check on her niece. She knocked on the door gently and opened it to find Amy lying on the bed, crying.

'If you are that scared of horses, Amy,' she said softly, 'then it's time to overcome your fears. Melly is still waiting, and I'm not unsaddling her until you get on her. It's up to you. You can make her spend a very uncomfortable day at the back door waiting for you or go out and have a small ride so that she can be unsaddled and released. Do you want that nice horse standing there all day because you are scared to get on her?'

'I'm not scared,' Amy said between sniffs.

'Then come out and get on her. Just walk with Matthew down to the cattle yards and back.'

After a few more minutes, Mrs. Winter managed to get Amy back to the horse and showed her how to put the reins over Melly's neck.

'Just put your foot in the stirrup and see if you can swing on board. Matthew will show you.'

Matthew dismounted and mounted a couple of times as a demonstration before Amy put her right foot in the stirrup and went to mount.

'I wouldn't do that,' Matthew told her with a chuckle,

shaking his head over the fact that his cousin hadn't been able to see that he used his left foot to mount. 'If you get up with the right foot in the stirrup, you'll end up backward in the saddle. You have to use your left foot.'

Amy swapped feet and then scrambled aboard, hanging off the side of the saddle for a few moments before collapsing into it like a bag of mud. She picked up the reins, holding them up near her chest. Matthew explained where she should hold them and told her to sit up straight and push her weight down into her stirrups.

'Think of holding your height up through your head, your shoulders back, and your weight down into your heels,' Matthew told her as they began walking slowly away from the house, repeating lessons he'd heard all his life.

Amy grabbed at the saddle at first but then seemed to adjust to the walking motion. She lifted her left hand and swung it out wide so that Melly turned a small circle to the left before ending up back facing the cattle yards again.

'I turned her,' Amy said, appearing proud of herself.

'Good on you,' Matthew sounded genuinely pleased for her and encouraged her, which surprised her after the way she'd been treating him for the past few days. 'Next time, you can just do this,' he demonstrated much smaller movements with his reins. 'Think, *turn left* and feel the rein lightly; you don't even have to pull it. You tilt your wrist under like this without moving your arm, and she'll turn. She's got a good mouth.'

Amy practiced turning to the right with the smaller action that Matthew demonstrated. When she pulled the reins back behind her body to stop Melly, Matthew explained how to keep her hands in front of the saddle and use the reins from that position. By the time they reached the cattle yards, Amy was able to ask Melly to walk, stop, and turn. Matthew checked the water troughs in the yards and made sure that the cattle had plenty of hay in their feeders, and they walked back to the house.

Despite her objections to having anything to do with horses, Amy found that she enjoyed sitting on Melly walking down a dusty outback road with her cousin. The horizon stretched around them, uncluttered by buildings, power poles, or any of the city chaos. In front of them, the homestead and buildings looked like an oasis in the expanse of brown. Behind the homestead was a line of hills about forty kilometers long, the Sunhaven Hills, and they made an impressive backdrop to the house. Amy found herself enjoying the view as the clip-clop of hooves on the road tapped out a comforting rhythm.

'Want to try a trot?' asked Matthew. 'It's faster and bumpier, and if I say *up down up down* to Melly's steps, and you stand up in your stirrups for *up* and sit in the saddle for *down*, the bumps will go away, and you'll be rising to the trot.'

Amy shrugged, 'I'll give it a go.'

Matthew's horse trotted slowly as he encouraged Melly to trot. He counted the ups and downs out loud as Amy flopped around in the saddle, leaning to the left, swaying to the right, and bending forward over the front of the saddle, but never once actually rising to the trot. After about twenty meters of this, Matthew made some choking noises. Amy looked at him, seeing his face red and strained as he tried not to laugh. His face was breaking under the strain of holding it in, and she couldn't help herself - she giggled. That set Matthew off, and, unable to stop, he burst into uncontrollable laughter, doubling up in the saddle as he laughed till tears rolled down his cheeks. Amy pulled Melly back to a walk and joined her cousin in the amusement at the picture she presented in the saddle.

'Did I really look that bad?' she asked between chortles.

'Worse,' he howled. 'I've never seen anyone so bad… you were wobbling around like a jellyfish. I have no idea how you managed to stay in the saddle.'

'I was hanging on,' she admitted.

'You'd better hang on,' he chuckled, 'because there's nothing else keeping you in the saddle. Gravity is your enemy.'

'Melly was good to put up with me.'

'Yeah, she's the best. She taught us all to ride, and she puts up with anything. Want to go for another ride tomorrow?'

Amy almost turned the offer down, then realized how much she had enjoyed being on Melly and seeing the land from the top of a horse, and she agreed. I know it's a bad move, she told herself, but I can't help myself; I want to do this - I'll face the problems when they happen.

CHAPTER SIX
The Min Min Lights

The following day, Amy followed Matthew out to the stables to help catch and saddle Melly. Dane and Lani were already on their horses doing some jumping. A set of jumps set at about a meter in height dotted the riding arena, and they cantered their horses calmly around the course, clearing every jump cleanly and neatly.

'We have the pony club gymkhana at the end of the holidays,' Matthew explained. 'We compete in all the classes. Dane and Lani compete against each other, so it's always a battle to see which one wins.'

'Doesn't anyone else stand a chance?'

'Against my brother and sister? Not a chance. They are the best of the best with honors around here. Oh, except for, maybe, Mahalia Wren and Brandon Suffolk. They're pretty good, too. You'll meet them at the gymkhana. I usually win my age level, too, but I don't care that much about winning. Lani and Dane love to win.'

'I can understand that,' she said thoughtfully as she

43

watched them circle their horses and take the course one more time.

'Do you want to meet the other horses?' Matthew asked her.

'Not really, but knock yourself out and make the introductions.'

'This is Captain; he's Mum's polocrosse horse,' Matthew patted the black neck as the horse stretched out to sniff him. 'Lani's horse is called Fleet, and Dane rides Misty. They have other horses, but they're the main competition ones. I ride Shandy. Dad rides this big grey horse, Smoke, but he's not very quiet, and he bites, so stay away from him. He was crazy when Dad bought him. His owners were going to shoot him, but Dad has him going sweet now; you just have to stay out of range of his teeth. There are about twenty other riding horses out in this paddock, but it's two thousand hectares, so you probably haven't seen them since you've been here.'

Amy looked at a yard and stable set off by themselves past the riding arena and saw a big chestnut horse standing in the shade of a tree that hung over the yard. 'Who's that horse?' she pointed at the chestnut.

'That's Lord Sunhaven – we call him Laddie. He's our racehorse, or he will be when he settles down. Dad's the only one who can ride him – he's super-fast, but he can buck like a bronco, and no jockeys could ride him. He's five years old now and still hasn't raced, but Dad hopes he'll be sensible enough to race this year. I think Dad should sell him because he's dangerous; he's too hot between the ears.'

Amy smiled at her younger cousin. He was only ten, but he talked like he was an old man who'd been around forever.

After Matthew showed Amy how to put the saddle on the right way and fixed all the mistakes she made when she tried to do it herself, he saddled his horse, and they set out for a walk down the road. The other two watched them ride away, cast each other a questioning look, then cantered after them.

'Can we come?' Lani asked.

'As long as you don't laugh too much at me,' Amy replied.

'Nah, I think you're brave getting on a horse if you're scared of them.'

'I never said I was scared of them,' Amy pointed out, arching an eyebrow at her cousin.

'Then try a trot,' Lani challenged her.

'This, you've gotta see,' Matthew laughed without malice. 'Amy can swing around in that saddle like she's broken at the waist, and she sticks there like a champion, I tell you, she's going to be an awesome rider.'

Amy clutched her reins, leaned forward over the saddle, and urged Melly into a slow trot, bouncing around in what seemed an amazing defiance of gravity.

Matthew chanted *up down, up, down, up, down*, as they trotted along, but Amy didn't seem to get the hang of rising out of the saddle and sitting again; she just swayed around happily. Lani rode alongside her and gently took her arm, guiding her up and down by pushing her arm up and down at the right time. On the other side, Dane explained that she should sit up straight rather than lean so far forward. Between the three of them helping her, she began to pick up the beat and rise to the trot.

They had covered several hundred meters at the trot when a mob of feral goats suddenly raced out of the bushes at the side of the track and ran in front of them, causing the horses to prop in alarm. The stink of the billy goats hit the horses' nostrils, and they reacted violently to the smell. Matthew was almost unseated as his horse spun around in horror. Fleet, with Lani on board, ran backward and began to buck. Both Misty and Melly reared.

Dane tried to grab at his cousin as Melly went up on her hind legs, knowing that she could end up pulling her horse over backward if she pulled on the reins, but Misty twisted while she was up on her hind legs, and he had to grab for her neck to stay on board. Out of the corner of his eye, he saw his cousin lean forward as Melly, normally so placid, joined the other horses in their panic and reared high on her back legs before dropping to the ground and standing calmly. Amy stayed in the saddle as if she'd been born to it. He realized, with surprise, that she had the makings of a top rider.

'You OK?' Lani asked Amy once she had Fleet settled down. 'Melly doesn't usually do anything wrong when she has a beginner on her, so sorry she reared like that.'

'Amy didn't even move,' said Dane with admiration in his voice. 'I swear, she just sat there like she was glued to the saddle.'

'I used to do gymnastics,' explained Amy, looking embarrassed. 'I have good balance.'

'Just as well,' grinned Matthew, 'if you wobble around in the saddle like this at the trot, you're going to need all your gymnastics training when you start to canter.'

'If I keep riding,' said Amy.

'How can you give this up once you've started? Look at all this,' Dane pointed at the line of hills that reared up out of the plains with rocky, shadowed sides and patches of trees.' The Sunhaven Hills are only a twenty-minute ride away if you trot and canter. You could ride over those hills all your life and never discover everything. On the back of a horse, you are the king of the world out here - or queen.'

'Wait till you're good enough to go for a ride by yourself,' said Lani. 'When you're out here all alone, just you and your horse, it's like nothing else you can imagine. It's like you, your horse, the sky, and the land are all joined up. I can't explain it, but you'll know the feeling when it happens.'

'Sounds a bit creepy,' Amy rolled her eyes.

'Creepy is when you're out here at night time, and you see the lights,' said Matthew.

'What lights?' Amy looked at him skeptically.

'The Min Min lights,' said Dane. 'I haven't seen them yet, but Dad's seen them a few times. He said they frightened him.'

'I thought the Min Min lights were just a made-up thing,' said Amy, relaxing to the easy walk of her horse as they continued along the dirt track towards the hills.

'They're real,' assured Lani. 'We've met lots of people who've seen them. And not the sort of people who make up stories, but normal people like us who really did see them. They swear that they're not swamp gas, car lights, the reflection of stars in a heat haze, or anything like that. The lights follow you in the dark, and they can jump from one side of you to the other without making a noise. They're creepy.'

'I sort of want to see them,' said Matthew, 'but I know how scared the people were who *did* see them, so I don't want that.'

'Well, add me to the list of people who don't want to see them,' Amy shook her head. 'They sound too spooky for me. Where did your Dad see them?'

'Once, between here and Winton,' Dane told her. 'He

was coming home from town late one night. It was around midnight, and he was about an hour from home when he saw some car lights out in the paddock next to him. The lights were facing him, but instead of coming closer, they went sideways, keeping pace with him. He stopped, and they looked like they were coming closer, so he got out to have a look. He said he couldn't hear a car; there was just a pair of headlights. Then, without making a noise, they jumped over the top of him and were on the other side of the road, still facing him like a pair of headlights or eyes. He got in his car and drove like mad, but he said the lights stayed out there next to him for the next twenty minutes, just watching him.'

Amy shuddered, 'That's pretty frightening.'

'Dad said it was terrifying. He had the shakes for days and wouldn't let any of us go out at night for months. He's seen them a few times up in the hills, too, but from a distance.'

Amy looked up at the flat-topped monolith that punched up from the plains. They suddenly seemed more ominous, looming over them, hiding the secrets of the Min Min lights.

Dane pointed at the center of the line of hills. 'Our Uncle John lives on the other side of Sunhaven Hills, and he's seen them. His house is straight over the hills from us. It takes over an hour to drive there around the road, but it's not far in a straight line over the hills. It'd take less than half an hour on a fast horse, but you can't make it all the way because of the gorge. And Uncle John reckons the Min Min lights like to hang around in that gorge.'

Matthew gave his cousin a sly look, 'If you keep learning how to ride, we'll take you there one day to have a look. You can only get there on horses unless you want to walk all the way.'

Raising her brows quizzically, Amy asked, 'And seeing a gorge that might be home to terrifying lights is supposed to make me want to keep riding?'

'Yeah, see your point,' laughed Matthew, realizing that it wasn't much of an incentive to learn how to ride, then he brightened, 'but it is worth seeing. Right at the very top is Legend's Leap, and that is awesome.'

Amy gave him a questioning look, and Lani took over the story. 'Legend's Leap is the narrowest part of the gorge; it's only about four meters across, just a narrow little section. If you're at the bottom during the day and look up, you can see stars. If you're at the top, it looks like a black gap cut through the ground. The gorge is wider on either side of the Leap, but that's the place where our great grandfather was supposed to have jumped his horse Legend across.'

'Four meters across?' Amy looked disbelieving.

'It's about two meters higher this side than the other, so I reckon it could be done,' put in Dane. 'Legend was supposed to be the best jumping horse in Queensland at the time, and our great grandfather told people that he could jump Sunhaven Gorge, so someone bet him a hundred pounds that he couldn't. There's about a twenty-meter run-up to the Leap, and I guess if he had Legend at full pace so he wouldn't stop, he could have made it. It's called Legend's Leap, so maybe it's true.'

'If he hadn't made it over, he'd have died,' added Lani. 'It's fifty meters straight down if he'd jumped short.'

'And it's not called Legend's Fall or Legend's Stop,' said Dane, his eyes crinkling with humor, 'so we figure he did make the leap.'

Matthew grinned at her, 'Do you want to come and see

Legend's Leap in a few days? You'll be able to ride well enough by then if you practice.'

Amy clicked Melly into a trot and clung to the saddle as she swayed along. 'Maybe,' she called back over her shoulder, 'as long as there aren't any Min Min lights hanging around.'

They rode for almost an hour. For the first time since Amy had arrived, they managed to talk to each other without her being rude to any of them or reminding them that Melbourne was so much better than life in the outback. Amy had been determined to remain sour towards her cousins, but there was something so pleasing about sitting on the back of a horse with the vastness of the land stretching around her that she found herself feeling happy for the first time in weeks. She even wondered if she should confess her secret to her cousins, but that would change everything, and she wasn't ready for that. Not yet.

That night, after going to her bedroom, Amy took out one of her suitcases from the wardrobe and carefully removed a scrapbook from the zip-up pocket inside. Checking that no one was about to enter her room, she returned to her bed and opened the book of photos, newspaper and magazine articles, and other mementos of her life before Sunhaven. Turning each page slowly, she savored the images and information from her past and tenderly touched some of the pieces stored in the beautifully decorated scrapbook. Tears began to run freely down her cheeks. She stopped her examination of her past and hugged the book to her chest, rocking on the bed as she cried about all she'd left behind.

CHAPTER SEVEN
Amy Rides Alone

Two days later, Amy asked her aunt if she could try going for a ride along the road to the first fence, over a kilometer away, and back by herself. Pleased to see her niece finally taking an interest in the outdoors and quite delighted to see her on a horse, Mrs. Winter helped her saddle Melly and sent her on her way. She had faith that the horse would look after Amy just as she'd cared for her children when she taught them to ride.

Amy walked for the first hundred meters. Breaking into a slow trot, she swayed in the saddle but managed to rise clumsily to the trot. After another hundred meters, she stopped and looked back at the house. All she could see was the top of the roof and the treetops. It would be impossible for anyone to see her unless they were standing on the roof of the house.

She looked around. There were no fences and no roads apart from the dirt track she was on. There was the dry

51

land sprinkled with green mimosa bushes and some tough trees. A kestrel hovered overhead, and a stream of zebra finches flowed past in the mimosa bushes, chirping madly as they flew. She was alone in the world with a good horse underneath her. Melly may have been quiet, but Amy knew she wasn't a plodder as she'd seen photos on her bedroom walls of her winning showjumping and dressage competitions with her cousins. She was a talented horse who just happened to be quiet for beginners.

Straightening in the saddle, Amy took a big breath of warm outback air and changed the angle of her hands and heels until she looked like her cousins in the saddle instead of a shaky beginner. Then she lightly squeezed Melly into a canter, and the horse responded quickly, tossing her head as she picked up speed along the road. Amy smiled to herself – she may have fooled her cousins with her bad riding, but the horse had always known she could ride.

Knowing that the fifteen-year-old mare was fit and well educated, Amy turned her off the road and headed across the paddock towards a fallen tree she'd watched her cousins jump the day before. It was only a meter high, but it was still a jump, and she felt Melly grow keen as soon as she realized what Amy intended.

Slowing Melly to a controlled canter, Amy closed her legs on her sides, making it clear that she wasn't to run left or right but was to go straight at the jump. In the last three strides, she pushed Melly forward so that they took off in the perfect position to sail easily over the jump, and, as they landed, she turned towards the creek. Cross country jumps were set up along the dry creek, and Amy threw her heart over every obstacle, carrying Melly with it. She was a brave horse who loved to jump, Amy had felt that from the moment she'd stepped into the saddle on that first day, and it was heaven to share the jumps with such a horse.

Together, they flew down and then up the sandy creek sides and over logs placed at the top, landing safely and taking two strides to bounce over a set of rails between two trees. They cantered along the top of the creek bank, dodging between trees until they came to a spread of brush and rails. She increased Melly's speed to clear the spread and landed a good meter from the far side. They turned to slide down the creek bank to the flat sandy bed, where there was room for three strides to prepare for a huge log lying across the creek. Amy felt the joy of flying over jumps surging through her, and she couldn't help the laughter that bubbled up. Nothing compared to the feeling of flying through the air on the back of a good horse.

The jumps weren't as challenging as the cross country courses at Werribee near her home or Gawler in South Australia, but it was amazing to be riding over jumps again. She realized she had been fooling herself when she intended to have nothing to do with horses until she found a way to get her horses back. She thought she couldn't live without her horses. Now, she realized that she couldn't live without any horses.

Walking Melly back towards the house to cool her before she arrived at the stables, Amy began to slump over and subtly turn her hands and legs until she once more looked like a beginner rider who was struggling with the basics.

'Have a good time?' asked her aunt as she helped Amy unsaddle and hose Melly down.

'It was great,' Amy smiled at her. 'Once you're out of sight of the house, you do feel like you're alone in the world.'

'So, do you feel up to riding to Legend's Leap with your

cousins tomorrow?'

'I'll give it a try. It sounds interesting.'

'I think you'll like it. I'll pack you all lunch, and you can make a day of it. There are a couple of orange trees growing near the gorge, so you'll have fruit to eat. They're the best oranges I've ever tasted. Your uncle says the Min Min grow them with magic.'

They put Melly in a yard with some hay and walked around the other horses. While Mrs. Winter was throwing some biscuits of hay to the mares and foals near the riding arena, Amy walked to Laddie's yard. He was the sort of horse that would make a great three-day event horse, bold and strong, with a shoulder sloped for jumping and a look of courage in his eye. Laddie walked over to the rails where Amy was standing and blew heavily out his nostrils at her. She smiled at him and stood her ground, knowing that he was deliberately trying to intimidate her.

Quickly glancing at her aunt to make sure she wasn't looking, she squared her shoulders towards the big gelding, raised a finger, and made a soft growling sound in her throat, taking a step towards the horse as she stared him in the eyes. Laddie recognized the body language of someone above him in the pecking order, lowered his head, and took a step back. Amy smiled at him and lowered her hand.

She was going to have to find a way to let the Winters know that she had deceived them about her riding abilities as she knew in her heart that she had to ride this horse. Laddie wasn't meant for a racetrack; he was made for galloping over jumps on a cross country course, performing dressage, and picking his way around a show jump course. He was the ultimate three-day eventer. He was the horse who could take her to the Olympics in six years, and she had to ride him.

CHAPTER EIGHT
Legend's Leap

The three teens and Matthew set out for Legend's Leap shortly after sunrise. The horses were fresh, and Mrs. Winter noticed that even Melly, who always dulled herself down to cater for a beginner rider, was tossing her head and dancing sideways. She looked more closely at her niece and saw her hunched over in the saddle like someone who couldn't ride. Her toes pointed down, and her hands were in the wrong position, but she had a good seat in the saddle. Even when Melly skittered sideways out of the way of Fleet, who gave a couple of bounds into the air demanding to get going, she didn't shift in the saddle.

Lani laughed at Fleet's high spirits, but Mrs. Winter was more interested in how Amy moved as though she was one with her horse despite the obvious signs of being a beginner rider. She watched them with a thoughtful expression on her face as they rode away towards the Sunhaven Hills. She hoped her sister made contact soon as she would like to ask her some questions.

'Almost one week of the holidays gone already,' said Lani as they trotted along, 'I wish we could stay on holidays forever.'

'It sucks that you guys have to go back to boarding school,' Matthew shook his head with mock sadness, then grinned, 'and I get to stay at home doing whatever I want.'

Dane reached over and slapped the back of his brother's helmet. 'Whatever you want, eh? Then how come I get emails from you during the term as you complain about all the school work you have to do and how much you wish were at school with me.'

'Just telling lies to make you feel better,' laughed Matthew, leaning away from his brother to avoid another helmet slap.

Amy found herself focussed on the word 'lies' and felt guilty about her lies. She tried to justify her actions by telling herself she didn't *actually* lie about not being able to ride. She had never said in so many words that she *couldn't* ride; they just assumed she couldn't ride. Pretending to be a beginner wasn't really lying, and she did it because she thought she would convince them to let her go back to Melbourne to stay with her friends without them ever learning that she was a horse person like them. She had wanted to make them dislike her so much that they would be pleased to see her leave. Liking her outback family had never figured in her plans, and now she felt stuck in her web of deceit.

'You'll like boarding school,' Lani informed her. 'I hated it at first because it was torture to be away from the horses, but that's not going to worry you, so you'll fit right in. Lots of city girls there, too, so you'll have more in common with them than with us.'

56

'I liked my old school,' said Amy truthfully. 'I wanted Mum to let me stay there to at least finish the year. It's going to be hard starting a new school for the last term of the year.'

'Yeah, why didn't they let you do that?' asked Dane.

'My stepfather, Nikos, is Greek, and he's obsessed with the importance of family. When he and Mum got a grant to do this dig in Turkey, he insisted that I stay with family, which is you. I wanted to stay with my friends, but he wouldn't have it.'

'Were you hoping we'd hate you so much that we'd send you back to your friends?' Lani guessed.

Amy laughed, 'I've been pretty hateful.'

'Not now that you're riding a horse,' Dane grinned at her. 'Do you think you're ready for a canter?'

Amy shrugged guiltily.

'Just lean back in the saddle and hang on to the pommel – the front of the saddle,' Matthew told her. 'It'll feel a bit frightening at first, but if you hang on tight and lean back a bit, after a while, you'll get the feel of it.'

'Melly won't take off no matter what you do wrong, and if you start falling, she'll just stop,' said Lani.

They moved their horses up into a slow canter. Amy let the reins hang loose and held the front of the saddle, swaying a bit to make it look like she was having trouble, but soon settled for sitting comfortably with just the bad set of her legs, hands, and shoulders making her look like a new rider. They cantered over the brown earth dotted with Mitchell grass tussocks, the horses picking their way easily over the ground which they'd traveled since being born. The sun shone warmly from its low position in the early morning sky, and there was not a cloud in the whole enormous blue dome.

'I think there are storms coming,' Dane surprised her with his announcement as they slowed to a walk.

'You're kidding, right?' Amy looked at him. 'I haven't seen a cloud since I've been here.'

'It's just a feeling in my bones,' he said in a wise voice, staring moodily at the horizon. He couldn't hold the serious expression for long and grinned, divulging the truth. 'I looked at the weather channel last night. There's a line of storms out in the Territory heading this way. They should be here in about two days.'

'I love storms,' said Lani.

'I can take them or leave them,' Amy shrugged. 'It's not something I've thought a lot about.'

'That's only because you've never seen one of our storms,' Lani told her. 'You stand outside on a starry night and watch the storm approaching. It's this giant cloud that glows with lightning. When it hits, you can't believe the lightning and the noise – you'll love them. Or hate them if you're scared of storms.'

'Are you scared of storms?' asked Matthew.

'They don't worry me,' replied Amy truthfully, 'but I still can't see how you can get a storm out of these skies.'

'Wait till tonight,' Dane assured her. 'The lightning will be in the distance. Tomorrow will be hot and humid, and tomorrow night the storms should nearly be here.'

They halted at a fence at the bottom of the Sunhaven Hills, and Dane dismounted to open a five-bar metal gate that had to be lifted slowly on its rusty hinges to open wide enough to ride through. Once they were in the hill paddock, he closed it behind them. The vegetation changed slightly as they rode towards the base of the hills, with more scrubby trees and rockier ground that grew clumps of spinifex grass. The spinifex looked green, and

Lani explained to Amy that it was always green, even in a drought, as it was a desert plant. In a fire, it burned with black smoke as though soaked in fuel.

As they began climbing the rocky track that led up the side of the hills, Amy could appreciate the size of the hills. From a distance, they looked long and flat and not very high, but as they walked and occasionally trotted up the narrow track, she realized that they were a small range of flat-topped mountains that reared up out of the plains country.

'Hundreds of millions of years ago, it would have been an island in the sea,' Dane explained, 'or a series of islands. You can find shell fossils around here. Down around the base of it, there have been some dinosaur fossils found. Sixty million years or so ago, it was probably more like a rain forest down on the plains.'

'You might need to lean forward on this next bit,' Lani told her. 'It's pretty steep, and if you lean forward, it frees up the back legs of the horses and makes it easier for them to climb.'

'And hang on,' added Matthew.

For almost thirty meters, the track was so steep that the horses strained hard to push upwards, then the ground began to level out again. After another couple of climbs, they reached the top of the Sunhaven Hills, and the three Winters turned their horses and gazed back over their land, knowing that the sight would awe their cousin.

It did. Amy looked out over a brown land that stretched so far away that it seemed to curve at the horizon where it met the sky. Far below, the colorful patchwork of Sunhaven homestead, with its scattering of red and silver rooves among the green gardens, was the only sign of humans in what seemed to be a vast ocean of pale brown.

Amy felt an awareness of being far from the sea, far from the edge of the ancient continent. Here, she was near the heart of her great land, and she thought she could hear the heartbeat.

'That's our place,' said Lani, looking across her land. 'And yours, too, if you stay here.'

'It's so big,' Amy shook her head at the landscape before her.

'It gets bigger further west,' said Dane, gazing into the distance, dreaming for a moment of being in the big country where properties were as large as small countries. 'We only have twenty thousand hectares, which is big compared to what people have closer to the coast, but it's nothing to what they have further out.'

Amy could tell from the look on his face that 'further out' was the place he wanted to be, the outback was in his blood, and he wanted the big, open spaces rather than the confines of a city.

They rode away from the edge towards the center of the hills, following a track that was wide enough for one horse at a time. Dane pointed to a mob of wild goats, but they weren't close enough to startle the horses. They saw quite a few solidly built, dark-coated kangaroos that the Winters called wallaroos. The bright red track was easy to see amongst the browns of the grasses and the green of the spinifex, and after a few hundred meters, they came to a clearing where they halted and dismounted.

'We never take the horses to the edge of the Leap,' Dane said, 'just in case.'

'I've always had nightmares about it,' confessed Lani. 'I'm on a horse, and it gets dragged by some invisible force to the edge of the Leap, and we get pulled over. It's scary enough on my own feet without worrying about Fleet taking fright and jumping off.'

'And Fleet would,' chuckled Matthew. 'He's a fruitcake.'

'He's a good horse,' Lani defended her four-legged friend. 'He's just a little bit complicated, that's all.'

'Complicated like a fruitcake,' joked Matthew.

'That's better than being a dull mud pudding-like Shandy,' Lani insulted Matthew's horse. 'The only thoughts that go through his head are food and more food.'

'At least that would stop him from falling over the edge of the Leap. There's no food there, so he's not interested in going to the edge. Your crazy Fleet would take fright at a falling leaf and fling himself off.'

'Fleet would make it to the other side,' Lani insisted.

Dane shook his head, 'Nah, he'd fall like a lump of lead.'

They hooked the horses' reins to the branches of some trees, loosened their girths, and ran their stirrups up to remind themselves about the loose girths. Walking slowly towards the edge of Legend's Leap, Lani stopped a good meter back from the edge, thinking of her nightmare. Dane, Matthew, and Amy went right to the edge and looked down into the black chasm. The far side was slightly below them and looked to be well over four meters away with a good flat landing surface for a horse if their great grandfather had jumped his horse, Legend, over it - but it looked terrifying.

'This is where he was supposed to jump,' said Dane. 'Everyone stood around here, and he drove Legend at the edge, and they made it over. He had to ride back home the long way as it's a one-way jump; no horse could make it back up the Leap.'

'I don't think any horse could make it down the Leap,' Matthew shook his head at the drop. 'Once they had an idea of what was here, they'd hit the brakes and either stop before the edge or end up going over and falling.'

They looked down into the darkness where Amy could make out some reflections. 'Is there water down there?'

Dane nodded. 'There are springs here in the hills. There's some good grazing in the gorge either side of this narrow bit, and even in this drought, there's still water, but it's too dangerous for the stock, so we keep them fenced out of the Hills Paddock.'

'It's for kangaroos, emus, dingoes, goats, and foxes,' Matthew looked around, 'and us when we come here. And echidnas – lots of echidnas here in the Hills. We'll take you to the bottom of the gorge some time. It takes a lot longer to reach as you have to ride to the end of the hills before you find the way in, but it's really interesting. There's the Galaxy Walk where the stars shine from the edges of the gorge, and the swimming is great.'

'It's creepy down there,' put in Lani from behind them. 'Even on the hottest day, it's cool, and the water is always freezing.'

'You get freaked out too easily,' scoffed Dane. 'We've been in there heaps of times and never seen the Min Min or anything that is scary. It's a great place, so don't listen to Lani.'

'Where's your uncle's place from here?' asked Amy, remembering them telling her about his house on the other side of the Hills.

'I'll show you,' offered Dane, heading off to the right. 'Follow if you dare.'

'I'll stay with the horses,' said Lani, knowing where he was going.

'Me too,' agreed Matthew.

'They're chickens,' laughed Dane. 'There's a perfectly

safe bridge.'

'Safe like a mad dog on a weak chain,' grimaced Matthew. 'You don't know when it's going to get you, but it will get you.'

Amy and Dane followed the edge of the gorge for about thirty meters until it began to widen, and both banks were at the same level. There, strung between trees on either side of the gorge, was a wire-rope bridge with a narrow base of boards. It looked dangerous, but Dane just pulled on the thick wire-rope strands to check them and stepped out onto the boards. He held the ropes on either side of his waist, walking carefully across the gap. Amy held her breath as he crossed, imagining him plummeting into the darkness below if the wires gave way, but it barely even wobbled as he crossed.

'Coming?'

She hesitated, then sighed away her fears and began walking with baby steps across the bridge, forcing herself to watch the far side and not look down. Pretending it was just a few planks and ropes laid on the ground helped her overcome her fear, but she knew if she looked down, she might freeze. Dane took her hand for the last few steps and helped her onto solid ground, his eyes full of admiration for her courage.

They walked a hundred meters along a track until it began winding down the side of the hill, and he pointed to a house about a kilometer distant. 'That's where Uncle John lives. The path winds left and right all the way down, it's pretty confusing, but we've walked it a few times. It takes us over an hour to drive there if we go around the hills. There are gates to open and shut, and it's a long way to around the end of the hills and back to Uncle John's place. I'll take you over there next week if you get over your fear of driving with me.'

'It's not far as the crow flies,' said Amy, looking back from where they'd come. 'If these hills weren't here, it would only be about five or six kilometers from house to house, wouldn't it?'

'Yeah. Sometimes Uncle John brings some horses up to this side, and we ride up, leave our horses on our side, cross the bridge, and take his horses down to his place. Lani won't do it anymore because she started getting creeped out by the bridge.'

'I can understand that,' Amy smiled. 'It's pretty scary.'

'Not many people are brave enough to cross it,' he nodded at her, making it clear that he was complimenting her on her courage, and she felt strangely pleased to win the approval of her cousin.

They returned to the others and ate morning tea while talking about Legend's Leap, school, and their favorite movies. Once finished, they tightened their girths, remounted, and explored their side of the gorge. Dane led them to a couple of orange trees hidden in the hills, with big, juicy oranges decorating the branches. They grabbed a couple each, eating them as they rode along, laughing at Matthew's lame jokes. They trotted home with Amy, still pretending she was a beginner rider, but her cousins didn't tease her or make her feel like she was slowing them down.

That night, Amy sat in bed, looking at the photos in her scrapbook of her two horses, Jack and Days, the loves of her life. They had been her best friends, her reason for getting up every morning, even though her mother wished she would find interests elsewhere. The photos showed her competing with them across Victoria and adjoining states, doing dressage, jumping, and cross country. There were photos of her smiling as she received trophies and doing a lap of honor with a garland and trophy rug on her horse. A magazine page stuck in the book declared, 'Amity Fielding- King – Young Rider of the Year', with a list of wins from that year.

In the back was a handwritten note of her plans for the future, which included a list of competitions where she hoped to compete with Jack and Days. Halfway down the page was a question mark for the horse's name she was yet to find who would take her to the Olympics. That was her dream, to represent Australia on the Three Day Event team at the Olympic Games. That was the dream her mother and Nikos had smashed.

Her mother, a scholar, did not share her sporting dream and felt Amy had become obsessed with horses. When she and Nikos had the opportunity to go overseas for a year on a university-funded dig, she sold Amy's horses without her knowledge and organized to send her to the outback family, where Kristy hoped she'd learn there was more to life than horses. As much as Amy loved her mother, she couldn't forgive her for that day three weeks ago when she came home from school and saw a horse float leaving with Jack and Days inside.

At that moment, all her dreams shattered. She stood in her school uniform watching her horses leaving in someone else's float, the realization that her mother had sold her horses hitting her like a sledgehammer. Running after the float, she screamed the names of her horses, begging the driver to stop. The unknown buyers ignored her. They turned onto the main road and sped away, leaving her standing in the driveway calling the names of her horses until her voice broke with tears. She fell to the ground, her heartbreaking into a thousand tiny pieces, as she watched strangers driving away with her horses.

Up until the day her mother sent her north, she refused to speak to her or Nikos. She was so distressed that she couldn't go to school and couldn't bear to see her horse-riding friends or even walk outside to where the empty stables haunted her with memories of her horses. Day after day, she felt sick with grief that ate at her. She couldn't believe that her mother and Nikos had no concept of how they had hurt her. Her anger at them had extended to the Winters, who didn't even know she could ride horses.

Her mother had not brought the subject up in her brief talks with her sister, Eleanor, and they had left for Turkey the day Amy arrived in Queensland, so there was no communicating until they established their camp and set up the satellite dish. Her mother objected to the internet being used as a social network when she saw it as a scientific device, and she wasn't a believer in constant communication when the 'no news is good news' practice required less effort. She wasn't likely to make contact and tell the Winters about her horses. No one would find out about her horse-riding past unless she told them, and she didn't know how she could tell them that she'd lied to them.

That day, riding in the Sunhaven Hills had been close to the perfect day, she thought. If only she had her horses rather than a borrowed one. If only she could canter and jump alongside her cousins rather than bump along like a beginner. She wanted to share the contents of her scrapbook with the Winters, but there was no way she could bring this up without appearing deceitful. There wasn't any way she could think of to explain why she'd tricked them all, but events were rushing at them, which would change their lives, break their hearts, and reveal the truth about Amity Fielding-King.

66

CHAPTER NINE
Before The Storm

Dane had been right about the coming storms. The day after they rode to Legend's Leap, the first line of fluffy white clouds appeared in the sky after lunch. Amy couldn't see how such small clouds could herald the coming of storms. She spent the afternoon watching her cousins, aunt, and uncle working their horses while she sat in the shade of the stable with a book. The book was open, but she didn't read much – she was more interested in the horses.

Aunt Eleanor and her cousins practiced polocrosse again. After some flatwork with his horse Smoke, Uncle Geoff joined them. Judging from the trophies in the house, they were top-level players. Dane had proudly told her that their mother had twice played for Queensland, and he played on an adult team even though he was officially a Junior. She had never played the game, but she decided that it looked a lot of fun and admired their skills.

Uncle Geoff put Smoke away, left his stock saddle on

67

the rail outside the stables, and took an all-purpose English saddle and bridle over to Laddie's yard. Amy put down her book to openly study the horse. Her uncle saddled the big chestnut and led him out of his yard before mounting him. He moved off in a big swinging walk around the rectangular riding arena, snorting at the four polocrosse horses that were still dashing around with their riders. Laddie began to trot and canter around the arena on light hooves that fairly danced across the sand.

Her uncle held him on a firm rein, and she could tell he was expecting trouble from the horse. He didn't have to wait for more than a few laps of the arena before he found it. Laddie propped without warning, digging his front hooves into the sand. Uncle Geoff touched his sides with the spurs, and, as soon as the horse felt them on his sides, he let out a grunt and launched skywards. He twisted as he bucked, landing stiff-legged. The spurs touched him again, and once more, he catapulted off the sand.

The others stopped their horses until Laddie settled back down. After a few more bucks, he swished his tail and trotted forward as though nothing had happened. Uncle Geoff patted his neck and laughed. From the height he'd reached while bucking, Amy knew she was right in suspecting that the horse could jump. After he'd done a few more circuits of the arena, she went over and leaned against the outside rail to watch.

'Does he jump?' she asked her uncle as he rode past.

He flashed a grin at her in reply and pointed Laddie at one of the meter-high jumps. Without any more encouragement, the horse leaped over it, landing lightly. He cantered a small circle and returned to clear the jump a second time. The horse was as agile as a cat and jumped with the ideal outline or bascule, and Amy was thrilled with what she'd seen. Her horses had her at the top of the eventing field for her age, but she dreamt of a horse that would take her to the World Equestrian Games and the Olympics, and she knew she was looking at him. There were just a few minor problems to overcome first, she mused wryly.

After they finished the chores for the day, they all sat on the lawn facing the west. The storms were approaching from the Northern Territory in the west, and, as Dane had promised, there were massive clouds on the horizon flashing away with more explosions of light than any fireworks Amy had ever seen. She sat with her family watching the storms and, as they talked and laughed, she felt a sense of contentment, almost of belonging, as she enjoyed the warm breeze on her face, the glorious blaze of stars overhead, and the distant glowing of thunderstorms.

The next morning dawned warm and humid, with the air so heavy that everyone seemed to be moving slower.

'It's oppressive,' muttered Aunt Eleanor as she wiped the sweat from her face on a paper towel. 'I love the storms, but the humidity that comes with it is too much.'

Amy smiled to herself as Uncle Geoff caught his wife by the waist and pulled her into his arms for a hug, 'Storm season is an exciting season.'

Mrs. Winter slapped his hand and called him a name before telling him to have his breakfast and then do something useful.

He laughed at her, 'I'm going to service the vehicles today – can you do without the car this morning?'

'This morning, I can,' she told him, 'but I want it this afternoon before the storms hit as I want to run some supplies over to John.'

'Great, I want to see him about something as well, so

it's a date,' he grinned at her, and she slapped his hand a second time.

Amy liked the way they played around. Her mother and Nikos were very serious and rarely joked; they always seemed to be studying books or writing reports or articles for other archaeologists. Her aunt and uncle reminded her of teenagers in love rather than older people who had grown used to each other.

'Can I come?' Matthew asked as he stuffed a huge spoonful of cereal into his mouth.

'If you improve your table manners, you can,' his father told him, scruffing his hair as he sat down, 'and if you help me with the vehicles this morning.'

'Sure thing,' Matthew grinned at him. He loved helping his father with mechanical work.

'What are you doing this morning?' Mrs. Winter asked her niece.

'Lani was going to show me the swimming hole in the creek.'

'Good idea – it's going to be stinking hot before those storms hit,' her aunt nodded. 'If you stay out after lunch, make sure you're home safe before the lightning arrives.'

'And don't forget hats and sunscreen,' added Uncle Geoff.

Everyone went about their work after breakfast. Amy had been happy to take on the job of feeding and watering the dogs and keeping their pens clean as she liked the Kelpies. Blaze, one of the young Kelpies, was her favorite. He had started to follow her around when she was outside, gazing at her adoringly with his yellow eyes. He often brought her a stick and waited for her to throw it for him. She also took over feeding the hens, or chooks as everyone called them, and collecting the eggs, though she took her time entering the chook pen after Uncle Geoff warned her about the big brown snake that he'd seen disappearing down a hole under the laying boxes. It seemed the Winters weren't worried about living with some of the most venomous snakes in the world, but Amy did not want to come face to face with one in the chook pen.

As the sun rose higher in the sky, the heat became almost unbearable. When Lani threw her a towel and invited her to go down to the creek, she was relieved to go swimming. Matthew and Dane were working with their father on vehicles in the shed, and they called out that they'd be down for a swim when they finished.

'The waterhole is spring-fed,' explained Lani as they crossed a hundred meters of parched ground between the house garden and the creek, 'so even when it's low like this in the drought, it's still good, clean water, and safe to swim in.'

'Not like that one,' Amy indicated one of the almost dry waterholes further down the creek covered in green slime.

'Not like that,' Lani agreed. She stopped at the top of the creek bank and looked down at the clear water, which had a bank of sand on one side and smooth slabs of grey rock surrounding the rest of it. The coolibah trees that lined the creek provided shade for the edges of the waterhole while an area about the size of an Olympic pool glistened in the sun. 'This hole never gets any drier than what it is now, but if we get these storms this afternoon, the whole creek will be a raging river – wait till you see it.'

'It seems a hundred degrees hotter today than a few days ago,' remarked Amy, using the towel to wipe sweat from her face after they scrambled down the creek bank to the water's edge.

'It's the build-up before the storms,' said Lani. 'It always feels like something bad is going to happen.'

They left their towels on a rock and tip-toed into the water. The top few inches of water was hot from the sun, but down at their toes, it was chillingly cold. They floated out on their backs into the center of the water hole, gazing up at the fluffy cumulus clouds that grew and vanished then grew back again.

'I love waiting for the storms,' sighed Lani as she watched the clouds.

'I've never spent time waiting for a storm,' said Amy.

'Stay out here long enough, and you will. After so many years of drought, when storms are coming, you pray that they're going to bring rain and not fires.'

'Fires?'

'The lightning strikes can start fires in dry grass if there isn't much rain. You can see a storm marching across the plains, and fire after fire starts up behind it as the lightning gets the grass burning. It looks pretty awesome, except that then everyone has to go out with the fire trucks and put the fires out.'

'Is that why your Dad is servicing the vehicles today?'

'Probably. Not that there's much grass to burn at the moment, so it probably won't matter.'

'Ugh!' Amy shuddered as something brushed past her feet. 'What's in the water with us? Something touched my foot.'

'Giant eels,' said Lani, then burst into laughter when she saw the look of horror on Amy's face. 'Joking – it's probably a fish.'

'Do they bite?'

'Not unless they think your toes are fat worms.'

'Great,' Amy grimaced and brought her toes up to the surface of hot water.

'They don't bite,' Lani assured her with a grin. 'Race you to the side!'

They spent an hour in the water before the boys arrived with whoops and giant splashing bomb dives into the water next to them. The middle of the day passed quickly as they rigged up a swing in the tree over the waterhole and took turns swinging out over the water and letting go, then swimming back to the edge for their next turn. Amy hadn't noticed how the fluffy clouds had changed into enormous thunderheads in the distance until Lani pointed them out.

'Storms away!' she called, pointing at the western sky.

'Time to get back to the house,' declared Dane after looking at the storms.

'Aw, they're still hours and hours away, let's stay,' said Matthew.

'There'll be things to do before the storm gets here,' argued Dane, 'so let's get going.'

'Race you all!' laughed Matthew, who had made his way closer to the bank than the others as they talked.

They swam to the sandy beach and laughed as they scrambled out, grabbed their towels, and took off up the paddock for the house. The storm was still far in the distance. The anvil-shaped top climbed ten kilometers into the sky and streamed out to one side of the storm. It was massive. The sun on one side of it made the clouds brilliantly white against the blue sky, while the other side was dark grey and murky green. Amy had never seen a cloud-like it. It made her shiver. It looked too powerful.

As they reached the house, Mr. Winter called to Matthew that they were leaving for Uncle John's place in five minutes as they wanted to get back before the storm hit. The storm was only a few hours away by his calculations, so they were in a hurry. He had instructions for the three staying behind to get all the chores done before the storm arrived.

'Dane, can you saddle Laddie up in about two hours when I'm on my way back?' he asked as he hung out the window of the four-wheel-drive car. 'If I have time, I want to give him a quick ride before the storm's here. I don't want to miss a day riding him when he's almost over that bucking nonsense.'

'No worries, Dad,' nodded Dane. 'Drive carefully. We'll get everything done.'

'I have faith in you,' Mr. Winter smiled warmly at his son, then included the girls in his smile to make it clear that the remark was for all of them. 'Always.'

Amy felt a slight pain in her chest as she watched her aunt and uncle drive away. They made her feel so loved, and she was letting them down by continuing her deception. She knew that she had to tell them the truth. She stood for several minutes watching the trail of dust marking the car's path along the track leading around Sunhaven Hills towards Uncle John's property.

'I have faith in you. Always.' The last words he said included her in their meaning. The words would stay with Amy for the rest of her life.

CHAPTER TEN
The Accident

It seemed to grow hotter in the last hours before the storm. As the monster cloud loomed closer and began making the air vibrate with its rumbling, the three teens on Sunhaven Station finished all the work for the day and waited. Dane had saddled and bridled Laddie and left him in a stable for his father, though he doubted there'd be time to ride him before the rain arrived. He debated lunging the horse for his father, but he knew how unpredictable Laddie could be, and he didn't want to set his training back.

They waited, and the storms marched closer. In the distance, the up and down strikes of lightning looked as though someone in the clouds was stabbing the ground with narrow sticks made of the sun.

'I hope they get home soon,' murmured Lani, two and a half hours after her parents and brother had left. 'This storm looks like a bad one. And it's still building.'

As she spoke, the power in the house stopped, the fridges and fans ground to a halt, and the two-way radio crackled into silence.

'Great,' Dane kicked the veranda post with annoyance, 'we're off power.'

'If we don't go back on in a few minutes, start the generator, Dane,' suggested Lani, then turned to Amy with a reassuring smile, though there was an edge of worry in her eyes that remained. 'We often go off power during storms, don't worry, it's just one of those outback things. Everyone has a generator to create power until the mains line is fixed.'

'Yeah, well, we have a problem - that's what Dad wanted to see Uncle John about,' said Dane. 'He picked up generator parts for us in town yesterday, and until we have them, the generator won't be starting.'

Lani shrugged, 'No matter, Dad will be back any minute with them, and he'll get it going before dark.'

'I may as well unsaddle Laddie, then,' he said, frowning. 'Dad won't have time to work him if he has to fix the generator.'

A bolt of lightning shot out of the leading edge of the cloud, spearing into the ground less than a kilometer away. The explosion of thunder that followed spooked the horses in the stable. Amy could hear one of the horses kicking at the stable door in alarm.

'That's just Laddie,' Dane told her, 'he hates storms, and we always lock him up, so he doesn't gallop through a fence – he goes a bit crazy.'

'Here come Mum and Dad!' Lani shouted as she saw the cloud of dust approaching at speed, feeling relieved that they would be home during the storm. 'I like storms, so I wasn't worried about being home alone, but I didn't want them to be bogged down on the road somewhere in the rain if they weren't able to beat it home.'

The three of them went to the edge of the garden to wait for their family to drive up, but another bolt of lightning nearby made them jump, and they ran back to the shelter of the veranda. The rain still seemed distant, but the lightning came from the very front edge of the storm. No one wanted to risk standing in the open with that sort of lightning smashing into the ground around them. The car came closer, moving at speed, and Dane grinned at his sister, imagining his mother in the passenger seat telling their father to slow down while Matthew in the back seat would be urging him to drive faster.

The car was less than one hundred meters away and about to enter the enclosure formed by the homestead and buildings and still traveling fast when lightning hit a tree at the side of the road just in front of the car. Blinding light shook their eyes as the lightning pulsed along the tree, exploding the base of it and throwing it sideways into the phone and radio tower. In a metallic screaming of twisting metal, both tower and tree came crashing down into the path of the car.

The next few seconds unfolded as though events were taking place outside of normal time - so fast and yet horrendously slow so that every millisecond crawled. The car swerved in one direction to avoid the falling tower and tree, then jerked back as the tires hit the ridge at the road's edge. The car left the road and sailed into the air.

Dane, Lani, and Amy watched in shock as the car rolled in the air. The horrified faces of Eleanor and Geoff were framed in the windows as their arms moved to cover their eyes. It landed on its roof in a burst of dust and an explosion of airbags, and rolled over onto its side, then spun upright onto the wheels again. It continued to roll several more times before hitting the back of one of the cottages and coming to a halt on the crushed roof; its tires pointed to the sky, still spinning with an unnerving whir in the silence.

Amy stood frozen to the spot, stunned by what she had witnessed. After the explosion of thunder and the crashing and grinding sounds as the tower collapsed and the car rolled, the quiet that followed was horrible. It was as though time stopped in silence for a moment, then she heard the anguished cries of Lani and Dane as they ran to the car. She followed them, feeling their cries tearing at her heart as she prayed for their family to be alive.

The tires were still spinning when they reached the car. Lani was crying out, 'Mum! Dad!' as she threw herself at the car to look through the crushed windows at the deflating airbags, and then she began to sob as she saw the blood on the windscreen and a still hand pressed against the glass. Amy landed on her knees next to Lani and saw the three unconscious faces in the car and blood. Lots of blood.

'We need to get them out in case it catches on fire,' Amy told Dane, who stood next to them, his face deathly white as he looked at the crumpled vehicle.

'It's diesel,' he said as he thought through their options, 'not likely to burn. If they're alive, we have to get them out carefully in case they've got back injuries.'

'They're alive!' Lani insisted. 'Of course, they're alive!'

Dane shook his head and dropped to his hands and knees to crawl up to the car, trying to avoid the broken glass from both the car and the back windows of the cottage. 'Mum! Can you hear me!' he shouted at the car. The bloodied hand on the windscreen moved slightly in response. 'We're going to get you out, OK?'

Some movement in the car's back seat indicated that

Matthew was alive, and a frightened cry soon followed.

'You're OK, Matty,' Lani called to him. 'Just stay calm, try not to move, and we'll get you out in a minute.'

Another lightning strike hit the other side of the house, flashing the late afternoon air with light and causing Laddie in the stable to kick his door even harder.

'Matthew?' Mrs. Winter's voice was faint. Coughing followed, and Amy saw blood splatter the windscreen as she coughed.

'We've got to get an ambulance,' Amy told her cousins. 'They're badly hurt.'

'There's no power,' Dane looked at her, anguish on his face because he knew how everything stacked against them. 'That means we don't have a phone or a two-way to call for help. The two-way in the truck is broken. The one in this car is history. We're cut off. There is no help.'

'We have to get them out,' Lani sobbed, her panic mixed with reason. 'Can you go back to the house for the first aid kit, Amy – the big one behind the kitchen door – and some towels and rope and some sheets. And pillows. And some doonas if you can carry them.'

Amy sprang to her feet and ran with fear on her heels to fetch everything required. She collected the items Lani listed, throwing them into the large garden wheelbarrow near the back door. By the time she arrived back, Dane had managed to pull most of the crushed, laminated screen out onto the ground. Both Matthew and Aunt Eleanor were groaning but managing some words. Uncle Geoff was still silent, the side of his head oozing dark blood that also seemed to be coming out of his nose and ears. Amy was disturbed by how dark the thick blood appeared against his deathly white skin.

Lani grabbed the doonas out of the barrow and laid

them over the glass, then she and Dane crawled halfway into the car to undo their mother's seat belt and try and let her slide down onto the doona without risking her back. She lay on her side, groaning, and the three of them managed to drag the doona out of the car and onto the dirt a few meters away. Lani began wiping the blood off her mother as she tearfully ordered her to stay still.

'I'll be alright,' she wheezed to Lani, squeezing her hand, using her nursing background to diagnose her injuries. 'Broken ribs, left side. I think one's pierced my lung. That's the blood.' She paused and coughed up some more blood. 'I can still breathe. Need oxygen.' She coughed again.

Dane stared at the bright frothy blood around his mother's mouth for a second. His eyes narrowed in thought about the oxygen; then, he turned to Amy. 'Do you know what the oxy-acetylene set looks like? The two gas bottles on a trolley in the car shed?'

Amy pictured the big metal bottles on wheels where Uncle Geoff had been working earlier that day and nodded. Before Dane could say anything else, she sprinted to get it, understanding that one of the bottles was pure oxygen, which is what her aunt needed.

As she ran back, dragging the bottles behind her on their trolley, she saw Matthew crawling out of the front of the car, calling for his mother.

'Mum's OK, Matty,' Lani tried to soothe him. 'It's just blood. She's fine.'

'Dad's not awake yet,' Matthew sobbed. 'Wake him up, Dane. Wake Dad up!'

'I will, Matty, let's get you out with Mum first. Where are you hurt?'

Dane quickly looked over Matthew's limbs but couldn't

find anything broken. He used the scissors out of the first aid kit to cut his shirt off and revealed the red, bruised line of the seat belt across his chest that had saved his life.

'I think I'm OK,' Matthew wiped the tears from his eyes. 'Help Mum and Dad.'

'You just lie there, then, you hear me?' Dane said to him. 'You stay there near Mum and don't try and move or anything. If you feel faint or sick, let us know. And let us know if you feel sleepy – that's important, right?'

Matthew nodded.

Dane pulled the oxygen bottle out of the set and pushed the acetylene bottle well out of the way. 'I've turned it on, Lani,' he told his sister, 'just hold it near Mum's mouth and nose, so she's getting some extra oxygen, and keep her still.'

'You need to take the truck to Uncle John's place and get help,' Lani looked at her brother tearfully. 'We need the Flying Doctor or the medivac chopper. They're going to die if we can't get help.'

'They're not going to die,' Dane replied with more certainty than he felt. 'And we can't leave yet. We have to get Dad out.'

Amy stood up and listened to Laddie kicking at his stable door. In a moment of revelation, it was as though all the pieces of the puzzle suddenly fell into place in her mind. It would take over an hour to drive to Uncle John's property so that they could use his phone or two-way to call for help. It would take less than half an hour in a straight line on a fast horse. The fastest horse on Sunhaven was Laddie, and she knew in her heart that he was the only horse that could jump Legend's Leap. Uncle Geoff had asked for Laddie to be saddled and bridled, ready for a quick ride when he returned, so the horse was ready to ride now. In the very depths of her soul, she knew that she and the big chestnut horse were destined to be together.

'Is Laddie still saddled?' she asked Dane.

He ignored her as he crawled into the car to try and free his father. Another blade of lightning cut through the air nearby, shaking the buildings with the thunder that followed.

'Dane!' she shouted at him, bending over and shaking his legs to make sure he would listen. 'Is Laddie still saddled?'

'Forget him,' he snapped at her, angry that she was thinking of the welfare of a horse when his family was dying around him. 'He can stay saddled all night. We have to get Dad out of here.'

'I'm going to take him and ride to Uncle John's,' she told him and Lani. 'You said it could be done in under half an hour - I'll do it in twenty.'

Dane swore at her and backed out of the car so that he could look at her, 'Don't be stupid, Amy. He'll kill you.'

'I can ride him,' she yelled back at him as she began to sprint towards the stables, ignoring the shouts of her cousins telling her to stop.

'We'll have a fourth person dying on us,' Dane cursed as he watched his cousin run away. He knew even he wasn't good enough to ride Laddie. The horse was too strong and unpredictable. Even if any of them could ride him, Legend's Leap would pull them up, and they'd have to leave the horse and run the last kilometer in the rough hill country on foot. It would end up taking as long as driving around the long way. He couldn't believe that Amy was so dense as to think she could ride that racehorse when she could barely ride old Melly.

His mother coughed and raised a hand to get the attention of her children, 'Let her go,' she whispered, tears in her eyes. 'She'll be able to ride him.'

'Mum, she's only cantered once or twice – even if she can manage to get on Laddie, as soon as he takes off, she'll be on the ground, or worse, caught in the stirrup and dragged, and Laddie will kill her.' He swore again, angry that his cousin could be so stupid as to think she'd be able to handle that horse. This was not a happy-ending movie where the princess jumps on the wild unicorn, and suddenly it is tame, he thought as he battled between the need to get his father out of the car and the need to stop his cousin adding to their problems by being injured by Laddie. This was a real horse that a beginner could not handle.

'No,' Eleanor smiled at him, her eyes shining with the belief that he could not understand. 'She'll be fine. She knows she can handle him.'

As his mother's words sunk in, he saw Amy leading the sweating, wide-eyed Laddie out of the stable. The horse spun in circles around her in terror of the storm, but she stood her ground and settled him. She quickly and expertly shortened the stirrups. In those few seconds, it registered with him that Amy was handling Laddie, moving around him calmly and confidently with the assured air of someone who was a born horseperson. She put the reins over his head and didn't even try to get her foot up into the stirrup; she just grabbed a handful of mane and vaulted into his saddle, landing lightly on Laddie's back and sitting securely as he plunged sideways, startled by the different feel of this rider.

Riding bareheaded and in sneakers, something she had never done before as helmets and riding boots were mandatory with her instructor in Victoria, she gathered up the reins and sent the horse at a canter over to the car

83

wreck. Dane and Lani gazed up at her in wonder as she controlled the huge horse with an easy seat and a light rein, appearing welded to the saddle as he tossed his head and danced about nervously.

'In less than twenty minutes,' she promised, 'I'll be calling the Flying Doctor for you. Have torches ready to guide the chopper in because it's going to be dark soon. OK?'

Without waiting for an answer, she turned the horse towards the road, leaned forward slightly, and released the reins. Laddie exploded forward, his hooves spraying dirt ten meters behind him as he accelerated into a full gallop. Amy leaned over the horse's neck, her heels still at his sides as she knew he needed no encouragement to gallop with the sights and sounds of the storm chasing him like the hounds of hell.

The horse underneath her was everything she knew he'd be, and he responded to her softer, spurless style of riding without once attempting to remove her from the saddle. He laid his ears back against the wind and stretched his nose out into it, and ran as she knew he could. At the site of the wrecked car, Amy had felt helpless. She didn't know much about first aid, and she couldn't drive a vehicle to go for help, but this was something she could do. She could ride as though the lives of her family depended on it. And with Legend's Leap ahead of her, the lives of both Laddie and herself depended on her ability to convince the horse to jump anything she threw her heart over.

CHAPTER ELEVEN
Lani Takes the Truck

6.00 – 6.15 pm At Sunhaven

'I knew she could ride,' Mrs. Winter whispered to her children as they watched Amy gallop away in the last rays of light from the sun, golden against the black clouds of the storm.

The storm was almost overhead and would soon block the light. It was expanding to fill the entire southern and western sky. Another bolt of lightning came out of the storm's leading edge, hitting a tree a few hundred meters from Laddie. The explosion of light and sound caused him to leap into the air, but Amy didn't shift in her seat. She really could ride.

'Mum,' Dane crawled back out of the car after trying to help his unconscious father and sat next to her, tears on his cheeks, 'I don't know how to get Dad out of the car. The seat has him jammed up against the steering wheel, and I don't even know if he's alive – that injury on his head,' his voice faltered, 'it's not just the skin that's cut,

85

Mum, I can see some broken bone there...Dad's broken his skull.' He sniffed and fought back a sob of helplessness. The situation was overwhelming.

Mrs. Winter struggled to smile at her son to reassure him, her voice wheezing, 'Just do what you can. You can only do what you can.' She closed her eyes; it was a struggle to stay awake.

'Move his seat back,' suggested Matthew from where he lay next to his mother, his eyes half-open, his face pale with shock.

Lani laid one of the doonas over her younger brother, remembering that people in shock needed to be kept warm, and squeezed her mother's hand, urging her to stay awake. She knew that accident victims shouldn't go to sleep.

'Good idea, bro,' Dane wiped a hand across his face to remove the tears. Gathering his courage once more, he crawled back to the car and groped around to find the driver's seat adjuster, forced the lever over, and pushed the seat back so that there was some room between his father and the steering wheel. Mr. Winter hung from the seat belt, his eyes closed, blood dripping from the wound on his temple where his head had slammed against the side window. Dane licked the back of his fingers and placed them under his father's nose, closing his eyes and silently praying until he could feel the very faint breath on his wet fingers. His father was still alive, but Dane eyed the protruding white shard of bone from his head injury with a sick feeling in his stomach.

'Here,' Lani passed him some bandages and a short length of board that had broken off the exterior of the cottage where the car had hit it, 'bandage his head and shoulders to the board to try and keep his spine straight.'

Working in the confined spaces of the crushed cabin of the car, Dane managed to strap his father's head, neck, and shoulders to the short board, then strained to push his weight up off the seat belt so he could unlock the clip and lower his unconscious body to the ceiling of the car, which was now the floor. He had a doona lying there and, once he inched his father onto the doona, he nodded to Lani so she could help drag him away from the car.

'Keep his spine straight,' whispered their mother. 'Take blood pressure, pulse, respiration,' she struggled for breath, 'and mine, and Matthew's…write it down…keep us awake.'

Pushing away the feelings of panic and powerlessness, both Lani and Dane spent the next few minutes doing what they could to make their parents and brother as comfortable as possible. They couldn't wake their father, and their mother kept drifting off to sleep. They knew that if medical help didn't arrive as soon as possible, they could lose them both. Matthew seemed to be coping, but he was so pale. They were worried that he could be bleeding internally.

'Take the truck to Uncle John's,' Dane told his sister after debating with himself about what they should do. It was ten minutes since Amy had left, and he knew they couldn't rely on her in case she fell or lost her way. As he looked at the speed of the storm approaching, he didn't think his cousin would have enough time to even make it to Sunhaven Hills, much less across the top before it hit. The departing promise from his cousin about reaching Uncle John's place in twenty minutes had to be disregarded as it couldn't be done. He just hoped she found a safe spot and waited the storm out rather than risk her own life by trying to ride or walk in the hills in those conditions.

He didn't want to take the truck himself and leave his sister here because he had to face the possibility that his parents could die, and he felt it was his responsibility to be there to accept that burden, not leave it to his sister. By sending her away, he was trying to protect her from helplessly watching as they passed away. He had considered sending her on a horse over Sunhaven Hills. Leaving a horse at the Leap, crossing the bridge on foot, and running to Uncle John's house might be faster than the truck, but he knew she could not beat the storm now. He wanted her protected from the elements in the truck, not trapped in the open on the hills.

'You're going to have to go to Uncle John's as Amy mightn't make it. Even if she gets to the top, by the time she stops at the Leap and runs the rest of the way on foot, you'd nearly be there in the truck.'

'I'll go,' she looked pleased to have something to do. 'I'll be quick.'

'If the storm hits, you'll have to stop – don't try and cross the creek if it comes down before you get there.'

'I'll get there before that,' she vowed.

Dane patted her shoulder, 'Drive carefully.'

At thirteen, Lani was a reliable driver like most youngsters on outback stations, and he had no concerns about her safety in the truck. She would either make it to Uncle John's or be forced to stay in a safe place along the road. Either way, she would not have to remain here watching their parents.

Lani nodded and, without saying anything else, she ran to the shed where the six-tonne truck sat, the keys in the ignition. She spent a couple of seconds with the key half turned to make sure the engine warmed, then turned it over so that that engine fired up. After clicking her seat belt in place, she drove out of the shed and went slowly past her brother, looking to see if he wanted anything. He waved her on her way, so she began slipping through the gears and sped up along the road, hoping to get as far as possible before the rain hit and turned the road into mud.

Like most children who grew up on outback properties, she had been driving since she could reach the pedals with her feet, but she'd never had to drive with the stress of feeling that her family's lives depended on it. She knew it would take an hour to reach her uncle's house, probably more as she didn't have anyone with her to open the gates, and the day was ending quickly with only another fifteen minutes or so before the sunset. She hoped that Amy did make it there sooner, but twenty minutes? She shook her head. It couldn't be done unless she jumped Legend's Leap, and no one could do that.

CHAPTER TWELVE
Gallop To Legend's Leap

Amy 6.00 – 6.10 pm

The lightning hit not far from them, and Laddie leaped high into the air at full gallop. Amy smiled as she rode the wild bound with ease. This horse could jump, and she knew he'd be able to clear the Leap if he trusted her. His hooves beat out the rhythm she loved as they raced along the road towards the Sunhaven Hills. She let him run with the fear of the storm in his heart. She knew that he would ignore any attempt to slow him at this point, so she just had to let him gallop.

After the first kilometer of unrestrained speed, Amy checked him gently as she felt he was ready to start listening to her. Laddie responded and slowed slightly. She guided him off the road and into the paddock for a shortcut to the gate that led to Sunhaven Hills. He was sure-footed in the grass as he'd grown up in this country and knew how to race across the rough terrain without stumbling.

There were a few cross country jumps set up in the paddock, and Amy knew she needed to get the feel of Laddie's jumping style before they reached the gorge where a bad jump could kill them. Moving at just below full gallop, she began measuring his stride and, when she felt confident that she knew the distance, aimed him at one of the fallen logs between her and the gate to the hills. When she judged the distance to be three strides out from the log, she pushed Laddie forward hard and gave his reins a light check to make sure he looked at the jump. When he was in the sweet spot for take-off, he tucked his front legs up and powered over the jump, landing without missing a beat. He pricked his ears, excited by the new experience of jumping at full speed.

Between them and the gate to the Hill Paddock was one more jump, and as she rode Laddie at it, she could feel the moment when he saw the jump. His muscles tightened, and his ears were giving the obstacle his full attention. This horse was born to jump.

'I need some of that attention,' she told Laddie and was rewarded by his near side ear flicking around to show her he was listening. 'OK boy, just hold your pace and, one, two, three, hup!' Amy counted his strides in and felt the soaring joy of a horse that had discovered the freedom of leaving the ground and flying.

The winds from the storm hit them when they landed, dropping the temperature ten degrees in seconds, from the heat of the day to the chill of a storm with hail in it. The day grew darker as the storm closed in, and lightning dazzled them every few seconds as the display of electricity grew in frequency and intensity. She had always been scared of riding in thunderstorms, but she found this exhilarating as they raced across the plains to save her family.

They continued to gallop towards the Hill Paddock, and soon, the five-bar gate came into sight. Amy had no intention of losing a minute or two by stopping to dismount and drag the gate open. Laddie could jump the gate. Knowing that it was a bit too high to jump at full pace, she began to slow him to a fast canter as they approached. She felt him start to hesitate beneath her when he saw the gate as his instinct was to stop at a gate.

'Not this time,' she told him and insisted he go forward. 'After a lifetime of stopping at gates, now you're going to jump one.'

In the last five strides, Laddie tried hard to stop, but Amy flicked his neck with the reins, dug her heels into his sides, and urged him on with her voice so that he kept going forward. Finally, trusting her, he released the brakes in the last stride and went up and over the gate, clearing the top of it with ease.

'Good boy,' Amy murmured to him, patting his neck on landing. 'You and I will ride for Australia one day, believe it.'

Once on the other side, Amy pushed him back up into a gallop over the last stretch of flat ground before reaching Sunhaven Hills. The setting sun hid behind the threatening bank of dark clouds, and the light was eerily dim as the storm closed in around them. The rain still held back, and Amy prayed it would remain dry until she reached the homestead on the other side of the hills because the steep country would be treacherous once wet. Also, jumping Legend's Leap would be impossible with the slippery ground.

She eyed the steep track that they'd followed at a walk and trot just a few days earlier, only now she was facing it at a hand gallop. Knowing this would tire his muscles out far more than racing over the flat paddocks, Amy let him slow down into a big canter as he bounded up the slope. She gave him his head and trusted him to look for rocks on the uneven ground as he drove his legs tirelessly up the side of hills, not once asking to stop. Even with his sides heaving from the effort of the climb, he kept his ears forward and needed no encouragement from his rider to keep giving his all in this race to save her family.

The lightning hit the hills every few seconds because they were the highest point in the surrounding land, and the electricity was drawn to the shortest path between the ground and the clouds. Amy was blinded for several strides after a strike lit the sky only a hundred meters from the path. She stared at its brilliance as it pulsated with energy, leaving her eyes filled with shadow and glaring light so that they were unable to see the path. Relying on Laddie to keep her safe, she let him follow the path without guidance until she could see again.

At the top of the hills, she felt too exposed to the lightning, and she pressed Laddie forward towards the Leap, hoping to escape this dangerous location as quickly as possible. She was aware of how tired he was beginning to feel and gasped when he stumbled for the first time, almost going to his knees and lurching hard to keep his legs under him. Knowing he had to have full use of his muscles to make it over the gorge at its narrowest point, she slowed him down to a walk for twenty strides, cringing at every flash of lightning. The brief walk wasn't enough to have him recover fully, but she hoped it might allow enough oxygen to pump to his muscles so that they could launch him over the chasm that split the hills in two.

They entered the flat clearing in front of Legend's Leap

at a trot, and Amy picked up the reins and glanced to the heavens to ask for strength. For a moment, she considered leaving Laddie behind, crossing the footbridge, and running down to the homestead, but she knew that it would take too much time on foot, time her family didn't have. They had to make the jump.

With just a twenty-meter run-up to Legend's Leap, Amy forced Laddie forward into a canter, slapping the reins down his shoulders to make him go faster. He lacked the explosive response that he began with ten minutes ago, but she knew he had the heart to keep going if she asked, and she asked. If he were to reach the other side of the gorge, he would need to be close to full gallop to help carry him across. Jumping a span of four meters required speed. Jumping four meters with an abyss below required more courage than most horses would have, as well as a great deal of speed.

With four strides to go, Amy felt him hesitate as he realized there was a gap between them and the trees on the far side of the clearing. She jammed her heels into his sides and urged him on with her voice. A split second later, at three strides out, she felt every muscle in his body start to register danger in front, and he began to stop. If he lost momentum now, they would not make it across the Leap, and there was no longer enough room to stop as they would skid over the edge and fall. She yelled at him to keep going and kicked his sides with her feet in a desperate attempt to keep him galloping.

Just before his last stride, he saw the chasm yawning blackly below, and he dug his hooves into the crumbly gravel at the edge of the precipice and began to skid. Amy felt fear pierce her heart as she realized he no longer had the speed to carry them across to the other side, but they could no longer stop this side safely. They would go over the edge. She stared into the blackness of Sunhaven Gorge and noticed two lights far below. The Min Min. She knew she was about to plummet down to them.

CHAPTER THIRTEEN
Time Runs Out

Lani 6.15 – 6.40pm

Lani drove the truck as fast as she could without risking a rollover on the turns. She would slow to take the bends then shift back through the gears to accelerate out of the corners and make up time. It was a long way around Sunhaven Hills to Uncle John's place along rough tracks, but if Amy didn't make it, then no message would get out. She didn't want her parents or brother to die as they lay waiting for help that never came. She wiped tears out of her eyes with the back of her hand and tried not to think about the three of them lying beside the wrecked car. Instead, she concentrated on driving.

There was still no rain on the windscreen, but the wind from the storm was blowing dust all around, and the day had grown so dark that she flicked on the headlights to help her see the road clearly. The lightning flashed on all sides, and she knew she was running out of time. Once the rain started, she would have to slow the truck down as the roads became slippery and turned to mud. If the mud became heavy, the truck would grind to a halt.

Dane 6.15 – 6.40 pm

After Dane watched the truck disappear, he eyed the storm warily. He could smell the rain, so he knew it wasn't far away.

'Mum, I'm going to get a shelter to cover you,' he told her, and she nodded. 'Dad's still unconscious, so if he comes to while I'm gone, tell him I'll be back in a minute.'

He glanced at his father, who lay as if dead; only a light rising and falling of his chest showed that he still clung to life. Next to them, Matthew looked at him with worried eyes.

'It's OK, bro,' Dane tried to grin at his brother to give him a sense that everything was under control. 'We've got Amy pulling a miracle riding trick heading to Uncle John's on Laddie, and Lani is going there in the truck. It won't be long until we get some help. Don't move – I'll be back with something to keep the rain off. Alright?'

Matthew tried to nod, but his eyes filled with tears as he felt overwhelmed with everything that was going wrong. 'I don't want to die, Dane.'

Dane leaned over and patted him on the arm, 'It's going to be alright, Matty – you're just a bit bruised like when you fell out of the tree last year. You're going to be fine. Don't move in case you have a broken rib or something minor like that. I won't be long.'

He didn't want to be away from his family for a second longer than necessary, so he ran as fast as he could back to the storage shed where they kept the camping gear. Putting tents aside as they had inbuilt floors, he pulled out a folding marquee with zip-on sides, which could be set up over his family to help keep them dry when the rain started.

It was heavy, but he managed to drag it back and started setting it up next to Matthew so he could talk to his brother as he worked. It was a difficult task as it usually took two or three people to assemble it, and he was alone. He hid his tears of frustration as he battled to raise the marquee a leg at a time, slowly extending it until he could fasten the roof. He dragged it over his family, hammered the tether lines into the ground, and zipped on the sides so that they were protected when the rain hit. The last light of the day was disappearing, and he set up battery-powered lanterns inside the marquee so they were well lit. He had spare batteries to keep them going through the night.

Once his family was safely under cover, Dane took some moments to look at Sunhaven Hills, now disappearing behind a solid wall of rain. He shook his head - even if Amy had managed to make it to the top on Laddie, which he doubted, the rain would ruin her chances of reaching Uncle John. She'd never experienced the sort of downpour that was hitting the hills. She would get lost in the wet, dark world of an outback storm where the rain could obscure everything more than ten meters away. It wouldn't take long, and the rain would reach the track where Lani was driving, and she would only have minutes before the road became slippery. Even older, more experienced drivers bogged vehicles in these sorts of storms.

He looked at his watch. Thirty minutes had passed since Amy galloped away on Laddie. If she had reached Legend's Leap, she would have left Laddie and crossed the bridge on foot. It would take her another twenty minutes to run down the path – the path she didn't know - to Uncle John's house. His shoulders slumped as he knew she wouldn't find her way in the dark and the rain. He doubted that he could find his way down the other side of the hills to Uncle John's place in these conditions, so there was no chance of Amy finding the right path that twisted left and right down the slopes.

With a heavy heart, he turned to check on his family. He took blood pressure, pulse, and respiration details from each of them and wrote them down like his mother had told him on the charts in the first aid kit. He didn't know much about medicine, but he thought that his mother's low yet stable blood pressure was a good sign, while Matthew's was slowly falling as though he was bleeding internally. His mother insisted it was simply because he was resting, but Dane wasn't sure. His father, Dane's vision blurred with tears as he wrote the figures down, his father was dying, and he didn't know what to do to save him.

The blood pressure monitor registered figures so low that he checked them twice and asked his mother to look at them. The look in her eyes as she read the figures told him more than her reassuring words. He had flicked through the first aid folder of notes, but a severe head injury like that was not something that he could treat with a first aid kit, and it seemed there was nothing to do but wait and pray.

Lani 6.40 – 6.50 pm

The windscreen wipers slapped busily but could not keep up with the torrential downpour. Lani leaned forward over the steering wheel and peered out at the small area of road lit by the headlights, but the rain reflected so much light that it was difficult to see more than a few meters ahead. The road was fast disappearing into a sheet of water, and it was difficult to make out where the edges became paddock. Water seemed to cover everything around her. The rain pounded the roof of the truck as though a hundred people stood outside, slapping it with their hands, and the thunder seemed to rumble constantly over the sound of the truck's motor.

It had been twenty-five minutes since she left the scene of the accident, and she wasn't even a third of the way to Uncle John's because of the rain. Tears of frustration began to well up in her eyes. She tried not to think of her parents and brother lying by the wrecked car, depending on her to bring help. The full force of the storm had hit the Sunhaven Hills before it reached her, so she knew Amy could not have made it through, and now it looked as though she was going to fail as well. She slowed to a crawl and fought the steering wheel to stay on the road as the truck began to slide to the left and right on the slippery surface.

'Don't get bogged, don't get bogged, don't get bogged,' she repeated to herself as she felt the wheels of the truck start to grind through the surface of the road, cutting deep tracks in the mud. The engine worked harder as the black soil began to clog up the wheels. Lani went to the lowest gear to keep the truck crawling forward.

As the seconds ticked away and the storm increased in intensity, she began to realize that her efforts were futile. It would only be a matter of minutes before the truck would bog down completely and not go any further. Even it didn't bog in the mud, this amount of rain would bring the water down out of the gorge, and she'd never make it across the creek which lay a few kilometers ahead.

A minute later, when the truck slid gently sideways into the drain at the side of the road and the wheels sunk into half a meter of soft silt mud, Lani put her head down on the steering wheel and sobbed. The truck wasn't going anywhere. The best driver in the outback couldn't get it out of such a position, and even if it was still on the road, she knew the creek ahead would be rising so fast that there was no way the truck would make it across. She had failed. She couldn't get help for her parents. They would die in this storm. She had failed them.

Turning the engine off, Lani curled up on the seat and cried with the helplessness of it all. There was nothing she could do. She couldn't even walk for help now as the creeks would be impassable. She was alone on the side of a deserted road in a storm that brought a reprieve from the drought but ensured her parents would die. And maybe Matthew, too. She cried harder as she thought of her brother.

Dane 6.40 – 6.50 pm

The rain buffeted the marquee, but it held, keeping them dry as the storm raged. The lanterns provided plenty of light inside the marquee so that he could check his family. Outside was black now, except for when lightning shuddered light through the rain. He offered water to Matthew and his mother and asked her if he should get them food or something else, but she shook her head and told him it would be better if they didn't eat anything yet.

Dane checked the watch he kept in his pocket. It was over forty minutes since Amy left and half an hour since Lani drove away. He wrapped his arms across his chest and sighed as he stared at the darkness of the storm that shrouded them and faced the tragic truth - they could not have beaten the storm. There was no help coming.

Even if Amy had made it to the Sunhaven Hills, he thought, the storm would have hit before she had made it to the top, and she would be disoriented and unable to continue. Lani would be bogged in the truck somewhere as the road turned to mud in rain like this. He hoped she hadn't made it to the creek crossing near the halfway point and driven in as it could become a killer in seconds, capable of washing a truck away. He didn't know what to do.

Dane went to his mother and knelt beside her. She smiled weakly at him, 'Don't worry, Dane, you're doing everything you can,' she whispered between ragged breaths. 'Sometimes, you must accept that what will be will be. There are some things we can't change, and we can only pray it turns out. If it doesn't, then we must accept that there's something in the plan of our lives that we are yet to understand.'

He laid a hand on her cool forehead, 'Are you going to be alright, Mum? I don't know,' he hesitated, his voice catching, 'I don't know if Dad will make it. I need you.'

'I'll always be here, sweetheart.' She closed her eyes for a moment, and Dane's heart stopped as he thought his mother had died, but she moved her hand to take his hand, and she squeezed to let him know she was still with him.

Matthew was looking worse but smiled bravely as his brother checked him.

'You always were lazy,' Dane joked softly with him, giving his arm the lightest of fake punches. 'Look at you, lying around when there's work to be done.'

'Mum always said there was nothing like lying in bed listening to the sound of the rain on the roof,' Matthew replied hoarsely with a brave show of humor.

'Well, you keep on lying there. Help won't be far away,' Dane lied and moved over to his father.

Geoff Winter lay still. His skin was beyond deathly white in the light of the lamps; it now looked almost blue.

Dane froze at the side of his father and fell to his knees, a sob in his throat, his heart hurting with a pain he'd never felt before. He had seen so many animals die during his life on Sunhaven, during droughts and when someone had to put an injured animal down, that he knew what he was seeing - there was no longer any life in his father.

Stretching a shaking hand out, he held it near his father's face but didn't feel strong enough to touch his skin. He held it there, centimeters from his cheek as he watched his father's chest, looking for a rise and fall of breathing. His chest did not move. Steeling himself for the touch of death, he rested his fingers on his father's face and felt the cooling of flesh that no longer had a spirit inside of keeping it fired with the energy of life.

Dane covered his mouth to hold back the sound of grief that threatened to rise out of him. He didn't want Matthew to know that their father had died. He had to bear this himself. He turned to look at his mother and saw her looking at him, a finger raised to her lips to urge him to remain quiet, casting her eyes to Matthew to show that she didn't want him to know. She had seen the head injury and had known her husband could not survive. She hoped that he would last until medical help arrived so that their son did not have to go through this.

'CPR?' Dane whispered to his mother. 'Should I do CPR?'

All her children were trained in cardio-pulmonary resuscitation, but Eleanor knew it would not help Geoff. She had been watching him and knew he'd died quite peacefully several minutes ago, and it would only serve to distress Dane to let him think that he could do anything to bring his father back.

'There was never anything you could do, darling,' she

whispered to him, knowing her words wouldn't carry to Matthew over the sounds of the storm. 'Your dad was gone from the time of the accident, and his body was simply shutting down. Don't let Matthew know - we'll all grieve together later. For now, you have to stay strong for your brother.'

'I didn't even get to say goodbye to him,' Dane cried softly. 'I didn't tell him I loved him.'

'Shh,' she patted his hand gently. 'He knows you loved him. This is why we love each other every day that we can because we never know when one of us has to leave. Close your eyes for a moment, and you'll still feel him here with you. You'll feel his hand on your shoulder. He'll always be with you when you need him.' She closed her own eyes and was aware of the strength of her husband still near her, his love still holding her, his voice telling her they would be safe.

'Will you be alright?' he looked at his mother through tear-hazed eyes. 'I don't think we'll get any help before morning.'

'Have faith,' she uttered.

'I'm trying, Mum, but it's not easy having faith on a night like this.'

'Dane, these are the nights when faith comes easily, as we have nothing else left.'

Lani 6.50 - 6.55 pm

Lani lay curled on the seat, crying uncontrollably over her failure to reach Uncle John. The rain still pounded on the roof of the truck, and she wished it would stop so that she could get a torch and start walking home. There was no going forward because of the flooded creek, but she could get back to Dane, get a horse, and make the journey over the hills.

That thought made her sit up. She could start walking back now. That was a good plan – better than lying in the truck doing nothing. She wouldn't get lost following the road, even in the storm. Grabbing a torch from the floor of the truck and pulling out a raincoat from behind the seat, she opened the door into the rain and stepped out, donning the raincoat as she went. The water was halfway up to her knees, but she was at the side of the road where the ground was lower. She only had to get to the center of the road where it was higher, and she was out of the water.

Looking around, she got her bearings and then began following the road back to the homestead, avoiding the deep rut marks she had cut into the road with the wheels of the truck. The rain started to ease as the center of the storm passed. She kept walking, and soon, the heavy rain gave way to drizzle. The light show and rumbling lumbered away across the plains.

As she walked, she began to have an eerie sense of being watched. She looked over her shoulder and saw nothing through in the darkness. She was imagining things.

After a few more steps, she had the feeling again. She switched the torch off and stopped, looking around. She saw the light over the road, far away on the other side of the truck. A vehicle? She looked at it and realized that the road where the light shone was bumpy and wound left and right so that car lights would be moving around all over the place. This light seemed to approach as though floating above the ground, unwavering as it sliced through the rain.

She clutched the torch to her chest as fear shot through her. The Min Min lights -they were coming for her. They took people, she knew, and the people were never seen again. Terror gripped her as the lights came closer and closer through the remains of the rain.

Dane 6.55 – 7 pm

'Are Mum and Dad still OK?' Matthew asked.

Dane moved to his side, 'Everything is OK, Matthew. We might have to spend the night here, but I'll get some proper mattresses soon, so you don't have to lie on the ground.'

'It is pretty hard,' Matthew grimaced. 'Has Dad woken up yet?'

Dane shook his head, 'No, he's still sleeping, but Mum isn't worried.'

'Good,' Matthew nodded slightly, accepting his brother's words without question.

Unzipping one part of the marquee sides, Dane gazed out at the storm which had passed over and moved to the east. He wondered if his cousin and sister had stayed safe during the storm. Lani was wise to the ways of outback storms and wouldn't risk her life by doing something stupid, but he was worried about his cousin.

Suddenly, he noticed the light in the sky, approaching from the road where Lani had driven. The stories of the Min Min lights flooded his mind – how they came to collect the dead, how they stole people away, how they collected souls. He told himself that the stories were nonsense, and it was probably just ball lightning floating in the paddocks. Maybe Lani had turned and was driving back to the homestead, and it was an optical illusion that was making the lights look as though they were floating in the air. He stared at them closely, feeling another shade of fear coloring his heart.

Lani 6.55 – 7 pm

The light came closer, staring straight at her as though it was coming just for her. Lani remained still, terrified of its approach and hoping it wouldn't notice her.

Then she heard it. Over the sound of the rain pattering on her raincoat, above the rumbling of the thunder, she heard it. And she burst into sobs of relief. It was a helicopter. The rescue chopper was coming. Amy had made it through.

Dane 7 pm

The light swayed to the left and then to the right, searching for something, and all at once, Dane knew what it was. The rescue chopper was looking for the lights Amy had told him to put out.

'Amy made it!' he shouted to Matthew and his mother, total relief surging through him. 'There's a chopper here!'

He raced out into the rain with a lantern and began waving it. He placed it on the ground and went back for several more from inside the marquee. He made a rough circle with the lanterns thirty meters from the marquee, big enough for the chopper to land. He stood outside the circle and continued to wave a lantern to bring the helicopter in.

CHAPTER FOURTEEN
The Min Min Arrive

Amy 6.10 – 6.18 pm

Laddie scrambled desperately to stop in that last stride. Amy clung to the saddle, trying not to go over his head, and she screamed at him to jump. She knew they were about to plunge to their deaths when a bolt of lightning ripped the air open just behind them, and Laddie bunched his muscles and launched. Although he had lost his momentum, she had underestimated the sheer jumping power of this horse. Once he spied the far side of the chasm, he leaped for it, soaring through the air with a mighty force. Amy leaned over his neck and hoped his jump would carry them to the other side.

Out of the corner of her eye, as they sailed over the gorge, she saw the two lights, like headlights, in the gorge below. She didn't turn to look as she knew any movement could unbalance Laddie, so she kept still in the saddle. In her peripheral vision, she noticed the eerie lights staring at her from the blackness far down in the blackness.

He landed, his hooves hitting the dirt on the far side with a heavy thud. For a moment, Amy thought his hind legs were too close to the edge, and he was going to slip backward, but he surged forward, away from the gorge. Amy let out a gasp of relief and patted his neck. She let him canter to the edge of the clearing before stopping him and collapsing on his mane to draw breath. For a few seconds, she had thought they were going to die, but Laddie's ability had carried them over, and now she had to finish the job of getting help for her family.

The storm was almost on her, and the light was dim. She strained her eyes to see the path that would lead to Uncle John's house. Several tracks led away from the clearing on this side of Legend's Leap, and she wasn't sure which was the right one. It had only been a few days since she stood here with Dane, and he had pointed the way to the house. It hadn't seemed very important at the time, and everything appeared different now as the dark storm smothered the light.

In the gloom of the ending day, twin lights appeared down the middle track and wavered between the trees, beckoning her with their mystical glow. Laddie snorted nervously. Two people with torches in the bush, she wondered, and another two down in the gorge? Unlikely. The Min Min lights beckoning her to her death? Also, unlikely. She shrugged and clicked Laddie forward towards the lights. She may as well take that path and hope that the lights were people out walking.

Laddie trotted forward over the rough, rocky ground, and every time there was a stretch of smoother track, she pushed him up into a fast canter. The lights seemed to hover ahead of her, ignoring her when she called to them yet guiding her. No matter how fast she traveled, they always seemed to be just another fifty or a hundred meters ahead of her.

The rain began to fall, and Amy realized that she was hopelessly lost. She was heading downhill and following some strange lights that could be leading her over the edge of a cliff for all she knew. She cantered towards the lights, and they disappeared then reappeared to her right, shining through the rain. Thinking she had little choice now but to follow them, she turned Laddie and went after the lights. Several more times, they blinked out and reappeared somewhere else, causing her to change direction. She wondered if they were leading her away from the homestead or guiding her, but since she had no idea where the house was, she continued to follow the lights through the punishing rain.

Laddie seemed to understand that she wanted to follow the lights as he began chasing them without her needing to direct him. As the rain came tumbling down, the girl and the horse followed the floating lights down the treacherous path on the side of the Sunhaven Hills.

The lights blinked out and didn't reappear. Amy looked around and tentatively rode another ten meters before stopping. Casting her gaze around, she caught sight of them further away this time, much fainter through the trees and grey curtain of rain. They seemed to have changed color and brightness. Staring at them, she realized she was no longer looking at Min Min lights. She was looking at house lights, nestled between the trees only a few hundred meters away.

For one last time, she urged the tired horse into a canter, and in the dark grey light of the dying day, lit by flashes of lightning, Laddie carried her through the rain to the house. When they reached the house fence, she threw herself off

111

him, left his reins over the fence, and ran to the house.

'Call the hospital!' she yelled as she ran into the house without bothering to knock.

Looking almost identical to his older brother, John Winter stared at the bedraggled, wet girl in alarm.

'Uncle Geoff, Aunt Eleanor, and Matthew had a car crash and are badly injured,' she told him, her words rushing over each other. 'There's no phone or radio at home – they need help!'

'Where are they?' he asked, reaching for the phone.

'Right at the homestead. They made it home and then...' Amy stopped, unable to say another word as a massive wave of emotions swept over her when she thought of the accident.

John wasted no time with questions and was on the phone immediately. He called a friend in Longreach who flew the rescue helicopter as he knew how to find Sunhaven. Hanging up, he dialed again, calling the hospital for medical assistance to come with the chopper.

Amy looked at the clock on the kitchen wall. It was 6:18 exactly – she had made the ride in less than twenty minutes, as she promised, and help was on the way. At that point, her legs gave way, and she fell to the floor, exhausted.

John gave her a worried look, picked her up, and carried her to a couch in the lounge room. 'You're worn out. Did you drive around or take a horse to the Leap and run down from there?'

She shook her head, 'I rode. Laddie is outside.'

'Laddie?' he wore an expression of astonishment as the meaning of her words sunk in, 'Geoff's Laddie? You jumped Legend's Leap?'

Amy nodded and struggled to get to her feet, 'I have to take care of him; he'll be exhausted.'

'You'll stay right where you are, I'll fix him up for you,' he knelt beside the couch and smiled as he put out his hand, 'I'm John Winter, by the way, and I'm guessing you're the city cousin, Amy, who's come to visit.'

Shaking his hand, Amy offered him a weak smile, 'That's me, Mr. Winter.'

'Well, first up, you can call me Uncle John, like your cousins do, and, secondly, you can tell me how a city girl like you came to be able to ride that crazy big horse of Geoff's over Legend's Leap without killing herself.'

'I've been showjumping and eventing for years, and he's a great horse,' she shrugged, wishing she could curl up and go to sleep and forget about the car accident and the blood and the worry about whether or not they were alright. 'Can we get back to Sunhaven somehow to help them?'

He shook his head, 'Rain like this will have the creek down, so we won't be going anywhere till morning. But don't worry, my mate Dave flies the rescue chopper, and he'll be there with the doctor in no time. There's nothing else we can do for now. Dane and Lani have their heads screwed on right. They're as good as adults in an emergency – better than many - so it will all work out fine. You sit there while I tend to that big red horse, and then I'll get you something to eat, and you can tell me how you managed to find your way here.'

'I followed the lights.'

John was halfway out the door, and her words made him stop, 'The lights?' He turned to look at her.

'I guess they were the Min Min lights. I saw them down in the gorge when Laddie and I jumped over it, and then they led me down the hills to here. I was lost, but they showed me the way.'

'Well, I'll be...' he muttered, astonished but not

disbelieving and determined to find out more about the lights once he came back inside.

Laddie was still standing in the rain outside the house yard; his head lowered as he fought the fatigue in his muscles. John led him to the stables near the house, unsaddled him, and quickly rubbed him down. He found a rug for him and his feed and water.

'You're one helluva horse, Laddie – who'd have thought you could jump Legend's Leap? That girl sure must be able to ride, eh?' Laddie snorted into his feed, more interested in eating than listening to John talking.

CHAPTER FIFTEEN
You Only Have Two Choices

The days following the accident passed in a blur for Amy. Her Aunt Eleanor was flown to Brisbane for five days until she was cleared to travel back to the Longreach Hospital. Matthew spent three days in the Longreach Hospital under observation before being discharged into Uncle John's care. John Winter moved to a house in town with Dane, Lani, and Amy so that the children could visit Matthew every day and then Eleanor when she came back.

John also organized his brother's funeral, a heartbreaking task, but he wanted to spare Eleanor as much grief as possible, so he tried to take care of it and let her focus on recovering. Neighbors cared for both Sunhaven and John's property while they were away and insisted that they forget about anything to do with the stations. They would make sure everything was fine until the family returned.

The story of Amy's ride on Laddie, their jump over Legend's Leap, and their experience with the Min Min lights spread quickly. Two television crews and several newspapers wanted the story, but Amy was too sad over her uncle's death and the suffering of her three cousins to speak to them. The media crews traveled to Sunhaven to film and photograph Legend's Leap, marveling at the distance and the courage it must have taken to gallop a horse at the gap between the hills. Amy didn't even read the newspaper stories about that night as she couldn't shake the overwhelming sense of sadness and loss of the last month. Her horses had been sold, she had left her home and friends, her mother had gone away for a year, and now her uncle had died, and she saw that her losses paled in comparison.

It also revived her memories of when her father, Brett King, had died five years earlier. Her parents had already divorced, so she only saw him on weekends and holidays if he wasn't overseas on one of his archaeological digs in South America. One afternoon, she came home from school, and her mother told her that her father had died in a rock slide as he explored some ruins in Columbia. It didn't seem real. They were just words.

There was no funeral for her father, just a memorial service that she wasn't allowed to attend in case it upset her. She hadn't seen him for two months before that day, and she had no real sense of his death. It was as though he had stayed overseas and would come home eventually like he always did. She had no chance to grieve, and now she was feeling all the sorrow for an uncle she had only just met, and her troubles about losing her horses seemed trivial. One day, she would buy other horses. Next year her mother would come home. But Uncle Geoff was gone forever, and she didn't know how to help her cousins cope with such an enormous loss.

116

The funeral of Geoff Winter was a huge affair, with close to a thousand people driving and flying in from around the state to say their goodbyes. Amy sat silently in the Church, her arm around Lani, who cried softly on her shoulder. Eleanor had left the hospital that morning but was still so weak that she couldn't stand for long. She sat on the other side of Lani, holding her hand throughout the ceremony. Next to her was Matthew, with Dane's arm protectively around his shoulders, both boys sitting stiffly upright, their grief etched on their faces as they cried for their father, their hero.

It was the first funeral that Amy had attended, and she stared at the front of the church where the coffin that held her uncle's body sat draped with flowers. She wished she could go back in time and change the events of that day. If only her aunt and uncle hadn't raced the storm for that trip to Uncle John's. If only they had been a few seconds earlier or later so that the tree hadn't landed in front of them and caused the accident. If only it was a horrid dream, and she could wake and go to breakfast in the Sunhaven kitchen with Uncle Geoff smiling at her and joking with her cousins.

Various people spoke about Uncle Geoff's life, and Amy saw how many people loved this man and would miss him. He had lived the life of a good man, he had helped many people, given generously to those around him, and he left behind many who mourned his loss. She wished she had more time to get to know him better.

John Winter stood and took his place at the front of the Church and cleared his throat. 'Geoff was one of the finest men I have ever known,' he began. 'We all know about his life, so I won't go over that again, but I do want to remind you of some of the things Geoff believed. He believed in family and friends. He said we should live every day with as much love as possible for our family and friends in case any day is our last day with them. He didn't get the chance to say goodbye to Eleanor, Dane, Lani, Matthew, Amy, me, or any of us, but every day of his life was given to us in love, so we never doubted what his farewell to us would be. He would have told us to go on loving each other in case any day is our last day.

'When times were tough, he always told me that we only have two choices: we can cope with it, or we can't cope with it, but not coping isn't an option, so we just have to cope. Only he used to add in a few swear words.' There were murmurs of laughter throughout the Church. 'I know we will all cope, as hard as it seems at present. If you close your eyes and feel with your heart, you'll know that Geoff is still here with us, still sitting there with his family. He's telling me not to get too mushy, and he's trying to tell Eleanor and the kids that he will always be there for them. He loved them too much to leave them completely. His body has ceased to work, but his spirit lives on. The great energy of spirit that was Geoff hasn't gone because energy doesn't just stop; it simply changes form. We won't see Geoff walking towards us, that lopsided grin on his face as he approaches, but our hearts will still know that he is with us.

'When you go home, think about the people around you. Forget your fights and differences, put away your anger and frustrations, and remember that these are the people you love and who love you, and they can be taken from you without warning at any time. Let them know that you love them.'

He continued, and Amy found some solace in his words. She had never before had to consider the deaths of people she loved because her mother had not discussed her father's death -he had just ceased to exist in her world. She realized the wisdom of Uncle John's words when he said to love family and friends as though any day could be the last day with them. She began to cry for her father, wishing she had been able to tell him that she had loved him, wishing that fathers did not leave their daughters to cope with growing up without them. Her arm tightened around Lani; it would be much worse for her cousin, she thought, as her father had been so much a part of her life rather than someone she spent occasional weekends with when he was available.

Some days after the funeral, they returned to Sunhaven Downs. The storms had transformed the browns and tans of the plains to a palette of delicious greens, and Amy was surprised at how different the paddocks looked covered in lush pasture rather than dead grass.

The neighbors had cleaned the accident site after the police investigation unit had finished with it, so it almost seemed as though everything was back to normal. It was almost like Uncle Geoff could come walking through the door at any moment. The neighbors took it upon themselves to keep coming over each day to do some of the chores around the station until the Winters managed to get back into their routine of station life without Geoff. Amy was amazed at the care everyone showed for the family as they struggled to continue without their husband and father.

'You need to start working your horses for the Pony Club Gymkhana,' Aunt Eleanor told the children the morning after they arrived home, ten days after the accident. 'There are only another five days until it's on, and you haven't missed one since the day you were able to hold yourself in a saddle.'

Dane shook his head, 'I think I'll skip it this year,' he moved some of the cereal in his bowl around, then pushed the bowl aside, uneaten. 'It just won't be the same without Dad.'

'Your father would want you to go,' his mother told him. 'You know he would. It's going to be hard for a while, but always ask yourself what Dad would want you to do - you'll know the answers.'

Amy sat quietly at the end of the table. Nothing had mentioned her deception about being able to ride. They had all thanked her numerous times for riding to Uncle John's for help that night, and they had marveled over her being able to cross Legend's Leap. They asked about the lights that had guided her down the other side of Sunhaven Hills and wondered about the nature of the Min Min. But Uncle Geoff's death had overshadowed everything, and they hadn't discussed why she had deceived them.

'Who would you like to ride, Amy?' Aunt Eleanor asked her. 'Melly will be fine if you want to take her, but now that we know you can ride better than any of us, you can have the pick of the horses.'

'I didn't mean to lie...' began Amy.

Her aunt raised a hand to stop her from going on, 'No need to apologize, Amy. In fact, I should apologize as the day before the accident I spoke to your neighbor down in Melbourne, and she explained about your riding and how your mother sold your horses, so I already knew. I understood what you were going through.' She wiped a hand across her forehead, 'Honestly, my sister might be smart, but she has all the sense of a dung beetle when it comes to people. Of course, you were so upset about having your horses sold that you pretended you hated horses, so you didn't have to have anything to do with them.'

'I don't blame you,' said Lani. 'If someone sold my horses, I'd be so cranky; I'd be the same.'

'You had me fooled,' Matthew smiled for the first time since the accident as he remembered the sight of Amy bouncing around on Melly's back, swaying around as though she was losing the battle with gravity. 'I kept wondering why you didn't just fall out of the saddle. You looked pretty crazy.'

'Did you play polocrosse in Victoria?' asked Dane.

Amy shook her head, 'Eventing, mainly. I have some photos if you'd like to see them.'

'We'd love to see,' Eleanor said kindly as her children nodded vigorously.

They sat around Amy as she went through her album, showing them her horses and some of the magazine articles.

'I've seen photos of Amity Fielding-King in horse magazines,' Lani laughed as she recognized the name. 'That's amazing that she is our Amy King... you're famous.'

Amy blushed, 'I'm not famous; I've just been lucky enough to have had some good photos taken.'

'So, this horse is Jack,' Matthew tapped one of the photos of a brown horse with Amy on board jumping an enormous log on a cross-country course. 'I like him. What breed is he?'

'Jack's full name is Gentleman Jack – his mother was a Thoroughbred, and his sire was a Warmblood. I've been competing on him for a year now, though I've had him for three years.'

'I love the Palomino,' Lani pointed at Amy's other

horse.

'That's First Days. I call him Days. He's out of a Thoroughbred mare too, and his dad is the Quarter Horse stallion, Days Of Gold. He's older than Jack. I've had him for about five years, and he's the best horse in the world.' Her eyes filled with tears as she looked at the photo of Days, then realized it must seem trivial to be crying over a horse when her cousins had lost their father; she would have to cope.

'I don't know why your mother wouldn't just send the horses up here for the year,' sniffed Eleanor disapprovingly, thinking that her bookish sister had never understood anything about how people loved their horses. 'I don't know what she was thinking, selling them on you like that.'

'She thought I'd get over them,' said Amy. 'She always thought horses were just a phase I was going through.'

Lani grinned and poked her cousin in the ribs, 'If it's in your blood, you're not going to get over it, ever.'

'It's not something you'll ever be able to control,' Mrs. Winter smiled at the four children. 'Your Dad always said that one day they'd find the gene responsible for it because it has to be genetic, this obsession we horse people have with our four-legged friends.' She was determined to continue talking about Geoff as normally as possible, so they didn't think it was acceptable to cope with loss by avoiding mentioning the one who had gone. She was sure her sister had done that when Amy's father had died.

'I know Mum couldn't understand it,' Amy sighed. 'My Dad – my real Dad, not my stepfather Nikos – he wasn't into horses either, but he knew that I was born loving them, so he made sure I was able to follow what I loved.'

'He died too, didn't he?' asked Matthew.

Amy shrugged, 'It doesn't feel like it – he just went to South America to a dig like he did every year, and he never came back. We didn't even have a funeral. He used to work away for one or two months of the year, and now it's like he's been away at work for five years. It doesn't feel any different from before, only longer.'

She felt guilty that she was experiencing more heartache for their father than her own, and somehow, Aunt Eleanor seemed to know what she was thinking. 'Grieving goes through several stages, Amy – first comes denial, and then you have to accept that the person you love is dead, that's why we have funerals and those official goodbyes around the coffin and grave. If your father wasn't brought back from South America, then you were never able to start the proper process of grieving. It's natural that you remain in that denial stage where you can't accept that he's gone.'

She paused to hug her niece and was relieved to feel her hugging back, unlike the unapproachable girl who had arrived some weeks ago, 'Sharing our loss of Geoff might help you come to terms about losing your dad. We're glad you're here to share this sad time with us because we all need to learn that the people we love can leave us, but we go on.'

After breakfast, they went outside to do their usual chores. Eleanor would continue running Sunhaven Downs, and they needed to form new routines, which included the tasks done by Geoff Winter. Uncle John was turning up each afternoon to help with anything that needed doing, and the workers who had been on holidays returned for the funeral and were back in residence on Sunhaven.

By mid-morning, they were saddling up their horses for some practice for their Pony Club gymkhana on the weekend. Amy had decided to take Melly as she knew she was a good competition horse, not just a beginner's mount. A gymkhana with sporting events, hacking, and rider classes wasn't a suitable event for a horse such as Laddie, so Amy didn't mention the possibility of taking him. Also, he was Uncle Geoff's horse, so she knew it wasn't appropriate to ask if she could ride him. Laddie was her long-term project, and she intended to speak to her aunt about riding him over the summer holidays when she came home from her first term at boarding school.

They practiced barrel racing, flag racing, bending poles, bounce poles, jumping, and hacking each day. Although the sadness over Geoff Winter's absence stayed with them, they laughed and enjoyed these times as they raced each other against the clock. They agreed that Amy and Melly were the best at jumping, but no one could beat Lani's slick times on Fleet around the barrels, and Matthew and Dane had the fastest times with the flags and bending poles. Most days, Eleanor sat watching them, sharing the moment with her husband, whom she was sure sat with her in spirit, watching their children.

This year, Eleanor was not competing. She usually won many senior events at the gymkhanas, but she decided to strap for the children and make sure their day was wonderful. Also, she was planning a formal thank you for Amy, which would take place at the Pony Club grounds. While the children rode, she would often go indoors to organize that while they couldn't listen in. As much as she loved her children, she knew they would not be able to keep the plans a secret from their cousin, so it was going to be a surprise for them as well.

During this time, Eleanor managed to contact her sister in Turkey. It had taken them longer than expected to set up their base camp and satellite phones, but at last, she was able to get news from home as well as a lecture from Eleanor about keeping Amy's talents secret. Amy spoke to her mother and, remembering Uncle John's words at the funeral, told her that she loved her, but the connection broke, and Amy wasn't sure if her mother had heard the words.

CHAPTER SIXTEEN
Thank You, Amy

'On you go, Melly,' Dane led the mare onto the gooseneck, tied her in place, then came out to help his mother close the tailgate.

'Great rig,' Amy admired the six-horse gooseneck, the name given to the large horse trailer that had living quarters in the front and required a truck to pull it.

'When we all play polocrosse, we need this for our five horses,' he hesitated, realizing his father's horse would no longer be included, then continued, 'and we take a spare horse that can be used as an umpire's horse as well.'

'Having beds, a fridge, and a microwave beats rolling swags on the ground, and this one even has a toilet and shower, so it is a home away from home,' Eleanor told her. 'Mind you, when Geoff and I used to play before the children were born, we just had a horse float pulled by our ute, and we slept in our swags on the back of the ute.'

Matthew came running up, tapping his watch, 'It's 4 am, Mum, and you said we'd be gone by now.'

'Thank you, Mr. Time Keeper,' she smiled at him. 'Everyone - into the truck, and we'll get going.'

As they drove over the dirt roads to the Pony Club grounds, almost two hours away, they played some of their favorite music, sang along with the songs they knew well, watched the sunrise, and talked about who would be there that day.

'Brandon Suffolk is a rodeo freak,' Dane told her about his friend. 'He doesn't walk around, he swaggers, and he always wants to wear these huge spurs,' he held his hands up as though measuring the size of a fish, 'and the instructors always tell him he can't wear them at Pony Club. He can ride any horse - nothing ever bucks him off.'

'And he's cute,' added Lani. 'Mahalia Wren is a polocrosse player like us, you'll like her, but her older sister Skye is so up herself that she drives us bonkers. It will kill her when she finds out how well you can ride and that you've been in magazines and everything. I'll make sure I tell her to Google you.'

'And wait till you meet all the O'Briens,' put in Matthew, 'there's like eight or nine of them, all on wild little horses that race around like mad blowflies. They're fun, but no one ever remembers all their names, and they all look alike.'

They continued telling Amy about what the day had in store for her in the way of people and horses and how the events would run. Time passed so quickly that they were soon pulling into the grounds marked by a few sheds, trees, arenas, and jumps in a paddock on someone's station. A pony club ground in the middle of nowhere is how it appeared to Amy.

They unloaded the horses and tied them up. Introductions began as more and more people came up to meet Amy. Most of them had been at Uncle Geoff's funeral, but there hadn't been the time to meet them that day, and they were all making up for it now. The names began running together in Amy's mind so she couldn't remember who was who, but they all seemed friendly and welcoming, and some of the adults grinned at her as they shook her hand as though they had a secret to share, and she began to find that annoying.

By eight o'clock, everyone seemed to be there, and Amy was surprised at the number. There appeared to be close to one hundred horses and several hundred people, along with a huge assortment of floats, trucks, and goosenecks filling the grounds. The announcer for the day was on the loudspeaker telling them that the scheduled start time was in forty minutes, 'And before the competition begins, folks, I want you all to come down to the main marshaling area for a special presentation before the first event kicks off.'

Leaving their horses tied to the side of the gooseneck, Amy went with her cousins to join the crowd at the yard in front of the sheds. They stood with Brandon, the rodeo boy who looked as though he should have had a rope in his hands and a bucking bull under him, and Mahalia, their fellow polocrosse player.

'We know this has been a tragic time,' the man on the microphone began, addressing the large audience around him, 'and we all want to let the Winters know how sorry we are for the loss of Geoff. He was a great man, and there isn't a person among us who has a bad thought about that man. But I'm not standing here to make everyone sad. I want to celebrate something very special.'

He paused, and Amy was suddenly aware that he was looking at her, 'Can Amy King come forward please.' She

129

instantly went red, but Lani and Dane gave her a shove. 'Come on out here, Amy, and let everyone have a look at you.'

Amy walked forward reluctantly to stand by the man. He put his hand out to shake hers, 'Pleasure to meet you, Amy,' he said as he shook her hand, 'I'm Michael Swanston.'

He continued to address the crowd, 'On the night of that accident on Sunhaven, the power was down, the communications tower was knocked out, and the roads became impassable with the storm. There seemed to be no way to get help, but this young lady mounted the fastest horse on the place, Lord Sunhaven, known as Laddie, and rode over the Sunhaven Hills to John Winter's house and raised the alarm. She not only rode over the hills, she also jumped Laddie across Legend's Leap.'

He paused to give everyone time to consider the magnitude of that jump. 'Many of us have visited that spot, wondering if the old story about jumping the horse called Legend over the gorge was true as it didn't seem possible, but Amy jumped Laddie over the Leap on the night of a storm, proving it could be done if you had enough courage.'

Everyone broke into spontaneous applause at that point, embarrassing Amy even further. Their faces looked at her with admiration, and she wished it could finish so that she could get on Melly and start riding.

'If it had not been for Amy's ride that night on Laddie, we might well have said goodbye to more than one of the Winters, and for that, the whole community is very thankful, but none more thankful than Eleanor Winter and Geoff's brother, John. Over the last week or so, they have been organizing a special thank you for Amy. It seemed like an impossible task to complete in under a month, but they managed to pull it off in the space of eight days with the help of many people from one end of Australia to the other, so here it is. Amy, your Aunt Eleanor, and John Winter want you to know just how much they appreciate what you did that night, and they'd like you to have this…'

Michael Swanston waved his hand to one side. Amy looked to see the crowd step apart as a new metallic gold truck drove slowly onto the grass behind them, pulling a matching gold gooseneck with the symbol of the sun painted on the front with the words, HORSES OF THE SUN inscribed across it. Along the side were the words, 'Amity Fielding-King – Eventing Rider.'

'They know you won't be driving it yourself for many years yet, but there'll always be someone available to drive for you, like John, who is behind the wheel right now.'

John Winter waved to her from the driver's seat.

Amy held her hand over her mouth, stunned by the gift. She had always traveled to competitions in her instructor's vehicle, and she had only ever dreamed of having her unit like this. She couldn't believe that Eleanor and John had bought it for her. She was about to step forward to go and inspect the gooseneck, but Michael's hand touched her shoulder to stop her.

'But what good is a gooseneck like this,' he announced to the crowd, 'without some good horses inside it?'

The tailgate dropped down, and Eleanor Winter led out a tall Palomino. Amy's heart did a backflip and then almost exploded into mad beating. It was Days. First Days was here. Her boy was here. She ran to him, tears flowing down her face, and threw her arms around his neck, burying her face into his white mane to breathe in the essence of the horse she loved. Days put his muzzle on her back and

131

whickered softly. The expression on his face made it clear to the onlookers that he knew who she was and was happy to be back with her.

Amy then flung her arms around Eleanor, 'I can't believe it,' she cried. 'Thank you, thank you, thank you!'

Eleanor smiled, 'No, thank *you*, Amy. You risked your life to save us, and this was the best way I could think of thanking you. Better get your other horse out now, though.'

She smiled as Amy looked up and noticed the second horse, Jack, standing in the gooseneck, waiting to step out. She cried his name and jumped into the gooseneck to lead him out into the sunshine, looking from one to the other, her heart bursting with joy over the reunion with her horses.

'They've been at my place for the last three days,' John came around and patted the two big horses. 'Their owners were only too happy to sell them back after they heard the whole story of how your mum sold them, and we had them trucked up here straight away. We thought you might like to choose one for the competition today. I haven't ridden either of them, but I've lunged them, so they should be fine for you to ride – they're fit and ready to go.'

'And you'll find all your gear in the gooseneck,' Eleanor told her. 'Your instructor gave me the list of everything you need for them, and it's all there, your saddles and bridles and even your competition clothes which your mum had put in storage. Quite a few people jumped in to help get this all organized, and between us all, it happened.'

'Thank you so much,' Amy fished a tissue out of her pocket to wipe away her tears. 'I never thought I'd see Days and Jack again. I don't know what to say; this is too much to take in...'

Michael Swanston stepped forward with the microphone, 'There's a bit more to take in as I think there's a couple of names here that we need to uncover so that Amy can see her team on display.'

Under her name along the side of the gooseneck, there were some wide strips of masking tape, and Mike tore the bottom piece of tape off, revealing the name *Gentleman Jack*. When he removed the next one, there was *First Days* written in matching script. Above his name, the third strip of tape was removed to expose the name *Lord Sunhaven*. When she saw Laddie's name, Amy caught her breath and looked to her aunt, who smiled at her.

'Everyone I spoke to in Victoria predicted that you would be riding for Australia before too long,' said Eleanor, 'and they told me that somewhere your Olympic horse was waiting for you. I was hoping that you might consider taking Laddie on. I can't think of anything that would make Geoff happier than to see his horse representing his country with his niece in the saddle, so I hope you don't mind that I added his name to your team. I know you have to go away to boarding school next week, but when you get home for the Christmas holidays, Laddie will be waiting to start work with you.'

'This is just too much,' Amy began, not knowing how she could ever thank her outback family. 'I don't deserve all this.'

'Yes, you do, Amy,' Dane stepped forward and gave her a brotherly slap on the back, grinning at her. 'You jumped Legend's Leap. You rode from house to house over the Sunhaven Hills in eighteen minutes. The Min Min lights helped you - that means you are awesome. This,' he waved a hand at the horses and the gooseneck, 'is what awesomeness deserves.'

Amy laughed with him, embarrassed by his praise but still swept up in the excitement of such wondrous gifts, 'How did you keep it a secret?'

Lani answered that with a wry glance at her mother, 'Easy – we didn't know about it until now. It's a surprise for us, too.'

With a grin, Matthew high-fived his mother. 'Good one, Mum – way to keep a secret! Don't tell the kids, eh?'

'I know you well enough to know that you'd have been bursting with hints for Amy from the moment you knew about it,' Eleanor Winter told him as she dropped a kiss on the top of his head. 'So, it was a secret from you all, but I think when you see the living quarters in the front of the gooseneck and the entertainment system there, you'll get over it. I'm sure you'll find that Amy will be willing to share her living quarters with family when we head away to some eventing days with her.'

'Oh, yeah!' Matthew exclaimed and headed to the door of the living quarters to inspect them.

The words, 'with family' echoed in Amy's head. The realization struck her that the Winters were her family. They loved her, they had faith in her, and Aunt Eleanor had done everything she could to put Amy's world back in its place, with her horses at her side and her dreams back where they belonged. This vast land that hugged her to its heart was now her home, and she felt, for the first time, that she truly belonged here.

Michael Swanston raised his microphone and announced, 'To Amity Fielding-King – our Amy. Our newest outback legend and, let me tell you, we're all going to be with you every step of the way as you start down that road to the Olympics. Let's hear it for our outback rider.'

The crowd began to clap, slowly at first, then built to

thunderous applause that startled some of the horses, though Jack and Days ignored it as they were used to the noise of crowds. Amy bowed her head, discomforted by the display. She wished they could hurry up and start the events so she could ride. People stepped forward to shake Amy's hand, hug Eleanor, and admire the horses and the gooseneck. Amy was relieved when the loudspeakers advised that there were only fifteen minutes to the first event, so everyone returned to their horses to finish saddling up and getting ready.

It was time to ride. Amy saddled up Days, leaving Jack tied to the gooseneck, and joined her three cousins as they warmed up their horses trotting around the main arena. Days towered over the outback horses, and his big elevated trot carried him so fast across the ground that Misty, Fleet, and Shandy had to break into a canter to keep up with him.

They pulled up at one end of the grounds, the four horses standing stirrup to stirrup, and they gazed back over the scene of horses and riders, floats, trucks, and cars coloring up the green fields.

'Ready to ride?' Dane asked the others.

'Always ready,' Lani grinned, 'We're the outback riders.'

'To us,' Matthew looked up at his cousin, 'The four outback riders.'

'To us,' Amy smiled at them. Her cousins, her family, her land. This was where she belonged.

ABOUT THE AUTHOR

Leanne Owens has spent most of her life around horses – riding, training, competing, breeding, and judging, as well as writing for horse magazines and writing and reporting for Horse Talk TV. She is an English teacher and spent many years in the outback, so it seemed natural to combine her knowledge of horses, teenagers, and the outback to write The Outback Riders series. Leanne has written many other books, including the popular Dimity Horse Mysteries which include the books MUTED and RESCUED. With many more books planned, Leanne has semi-retired from teaching to focus on her writing.

The Outback Riders series:
1 - Horses of the Sun
2 - Horses of the Light
3 - Horses of the Fire
4 - Horses of the Rain
5 - Horses of the Spirit

Other books by Leanne Owens
The Dimity Horse Mysteries
Book 1: Muted
Book 2: Rescued – Saving the Lost Horses

Flame the Fire Horse and Other Horse Stories
Star Writer – Finding Love Outside Her Books
Zo – She Loved Him for 500 Years

Made in the USA
Middletown, DE
04 October 2022